Come Rain

or

Come Shine

Come Rain

or

Come Shine

JAN KARON

G. P. PUTNAM'S SONS

NEW YORK

PUTNAM

G. P. PUTNAM'S SONS
Publishers Since 1838
An imprint of Penguin Random House LLC
375 Hudson Street
New York, New York 10014

Library of Congress Cataloging-in-Publication Data

Karon, Jan, date.
Come rain or come shine / Jan Karon.
p.   cm.
ISBN 978-0-399-16745-4 (hardcover)
I. Title.
PS3561.A678C59   2015   2015017803
813'.54—dc23

Printed in the United States of America
1   3   5   7   9   10   8   6   4   2

BOOK DESIGN BY AMANDA DEWEY

SAVE THE DATE, WEDDING INVITATION, AND
WEDDING PROGRAM COVER HAND-PAINTED BY MEIGHAN CAVANAUGH

COWS ON SAVE THE DATE DRAWN BY NANCY BASS

ENDPAPER PAINTED BY NANCY BASS

For Gracie

Come Rain

or

Come Shine

SAVE THE DATE

Lacey Harper Harper
&
Dooley Russell Kavanagh

THE BIG KNOT

Sunday, June 14

MEADOWGATE FARM

Farmer, North Carolina

One

'Hey, Dad. Need th' crimper.'

Crimper, snipper, stapler, strainer . . .

He was scrub nurse to the fence doctor, who was repairing a section of Meadowgate's high-tensile cattle fencing. Two of Dooley's five heifers had broken out last night and wandered into a neighbor's yard down the road. Not good.

'Glad it happened with the heifers. With Choo-Choo coming in a few weeks . . .'

'Don't want that big boy getting out,' he said.

'If he gets out, we're dead in the water. He'd head straight for Mink Hershell's cows.'

'Ah.' He didn't know much about those things.

'Mink's cows are small, he's got Dexters—around six, seven hundred pounds. Choo-Choo is two years old and clocks in at fourteen hundred pounds. He makes big calves, which can be a serious problem with a small breed. Mink could lose cows if our guy gets in his pasture. Dystocia.'

Life was happening fast. Dooley's graduation from vet school was coming up in a few weeks, then the bull delivery, then the practice turning over from Hal Owen, and on June fourteenth, the wedding . . .

'So how's Choo-Choo's disposition?'

'He's got calves all over the county. He's famous for gettin' the job done.'

'And you bought him because . . . ?'

'Not good timing, for sure, but the owner needed to let him go. It was me or somebody else. I could never top the price. Pliers.'

Tales about Choo-Choo were circulating at the co-op, at least one of them embellished with a direct warning.

'It'll be good to get out with your cattle in the evenings. Relaxing.' He was repeating what the neighbors said about having 'a few head' on the place.

'We'll treat small animals at th' clinic and I'll have my large-animal practice out here on th' back forty. I really wanted a mixed practice, but there's a great vet just a few miles north. She does it all and does it well.' Dooley wiped the sweat from his eyes. 'Hal loved doing it all, but he says he won't miss it; he was on call twenty-four/seven. I'd like to give it everything I've got during the day, and have time in the evenings to spend with Lace—with, you know . . .'

'Sure. With family. When you have children . . .'

He didn't mean to say that, not at all, it had popped out from overlong suppression.

The look on Dooley's face . . .

He had stepped in it, for sure. Craving grandkids was the vice of those wishing to assure mortality.

He let the air clear. 'So. Scared?'

Dooley gave him an ironic look. 'Were you scared?'

'I was. Then the peace flowed in.'

'Need th' crimper again,' said Dooley.

It was cool to know what this stuff was. He hauled the thing out of the workbox.

'Thanks, but that's the tamper.'

So this is what people called the simple life. He wiped his face with a bandana and went diving for the crimper.

Ever since they moved to Meadowgate a month ago, the entire household had gone hammer and tong making the old place ready for the Big Knot.

They had repainted the interior of the vet clinic, refinished the clinic floors, and installed new exam tables. He declined to help Cynthia and Lace make curtains for the farmhouse kitchen and drove with Harley to Holding to pick up a load of furniture for the reception room. Somewhere in there, he had conducted a house blessing and a clinic blessing, replete with thurible. Then came repairs on the barn and some minor work on the gutters of the house, and before Dooley wheeled in yesterday for the weekend, he and Harley and Willie had weed-whacked the fence line and had a serious conversation with the county agent about liming.

'It's your broomstraw,' said the agent.

'What about it?'

'It tells you your place needs lime. Nature's messenger.'

The agent had given him a wealth of material to read on the subject of lime.

For today's nut to crack, they were awarded the high-tensile-fence fix-off. He had prayed for a more challenging retirement, and here it was in living color. On the other hand, it was the most fun he'd had in a coon's age. Not everybody got to watch a young couple build a whole new life.

Lace Harper studied the canvas on the easel.

Being stuck happened a lot these days. Maybe she shouldn't be painting to focus her mind or clear it or whatever she was hoping to do. Maybe she should be painting for passion's sake or not at all.

But there was no passion in her—she was painting by a kind of rote. Every energy had lately been spent on this vast and overwhelming life they were entering, a life they had dreamed of for years and wanted with all their hearts—and now what had taken so long seemed so very sudden.

Suddenly their own kitchen with its amiable fireplace and big windows. Suddenly the old porches and creaking floors, the immense views, the enormous sky, the hundred acres, the doleful heifers with their grass breath—all theirs, and right next door, their own animal clinic. It seemed so grown-up to have a place like this.

A few years ago, Dooley and the trust people bought more land from Hal and Marge Owen. If cattle were to be in the picture, additional acreage would be needed and Hal made sure the price was right, as he'd done when Dooley bought out the practice.

Everybody had walked away happy, with the Owens keeping the remaining thirty-five acres. So now Hal and Marge and Rebecca Jane lived in the house they built on the hill to the south, and Hal would work part-time during Dooley's first year as a licensed doctor of veterinary medicine.

They were surrounded on every side by people older, wiser, and definitely more patient. This big new life seemed truly perfect—and also truly scary. The money Dooley inherited from Miss Sadie had stretched through his college and vet school years and bought the Meadowgate enterprise, with something left over. But there would be no tapping into the remainder of Miss Sadie's amazing trust, not for a long time.

All that lay ahead would be totally up to them. They had declined any further help from parents and would be living by their wits and on income from the clinic. It was important that the rest of the journey be theirs.

Bummer. She had no idea how to proceed with this painting. Maybe it was the subject itself. She was concocting apples from a cell phone photo and blurred imagination instead of working in plein air beneath a tree heavy with Winesaps.

But she wasn't trying to paint apples as God made them, she was painting at a slant—slathering on color with a palette knife, trying to chase the way the light was moving. All she really wanted was an impression of apples, an impression of a basket, an impression of mountains in the background. Anyway, it wasn't a real painting, it was an exercise.

She stepped away and squinted at the work. Clearly she was faking it. But she could not afford the time required to fake a painting, exercise or no.

Somehow she would make it work. Then maybe she could sell it. They needed money now, not just for the wedding, though it would be really, really simple, but also for the up-keep of the property and payroll for Willie and Harley and the clinic employees. Only days ago she had sold an oil to Cynthia's friend, Irene McGraw, who was a fabulous painter. She hoped Irene hadn't bought the small picture because she knew the 'kids' were just starting out. Irene had asked the price, but she asked Irene to price it instead.

'I can't do that,' Irene said in her quiet way.

She had blurted out the first thing that came to mind. 'Four hundred!' She didn't want to overestimate her work, not with Irene. At the same time, four hundred seemed overly modest. She felt awkward and gauche.

Irene smiled. 'You've forced me to set the price, after all. It's a wonderful piece. Twelve hundred.'

She had the sensation that she might fall backward, and held on to the chair where she was standing. She had sold a lot of work before, but this was especially thrilling because Irene McGraw's paintings were masterful.

The blood had beat in her again for the work she loved, the gorgeous work with its resinous smells and silken brushes and the restless play of light.

She should stop now. Time was precious. The Big Knot, as Harley called it, was only weeks away and Dooley's graduation at NC State was practically here, with the bull arriving the day after and the new sign for the vet clinic going up and . . .

She turned away from the canvas.

. . . and maybe, hopefully, please, God—Jack Tyler.

She felt her heart thump, something like a book dropped to the floor.

She and Dooley were taking on too much; everyone said that except Father Tim and Cynthia. Father Tim and Cynthia gave them all the liberty they needed, expecting them to do their best. Harley was the biggest objector. 'Th' way y'all are goin', you gon' be gray-headed.'

'Put your teeth in and have a Snickers,' she said. 'It's a *potluck*, Harley. Everybody brings food. It's the least stressful thing in the world, a potluck wedding.'

'Then there's ol' Choo-Choo comin' in,' said Harley. 'He's got ever'body on th' place rattled.'

True, but why was their bull everybody's business? People should be concentrating on the wedding, on getting the post in the ground for the new sign to be hung. Every time she went to Farmer, people were telling stories about this really mean bull named Choo-Choo—at the post office, the co-op, Jake's.

The grand wedding and honeymoon that her parents, Hoppy and Olivia, had hoped to give them would have eclipsed everything, bull included. She and Dooley were truly grateful, but they had to say they didn't want that.

7

She hated, hated to disappoint Olivia and Hoppy, who had been so eager to adopt her, Lace Turner, a total rebellious stray from the Creek who should be eager to please them and wear a gorgeous gown and have a wedding with all the frills at Lord's Chapel.

Olivia had come from a wealthy family. The silver-framed family portraits in all the rooms at Olivia's house were a testament to her paternal line of coal money. But the day she and Dooley went to tell them the plan, both Hoppy and Olivia had laughed with a kind of childlike delight. Olivia thought a country wedding would be 'the best thing in the whole world,' and the idea of a potluck was hilarious, but in a good way. 'It's not our wedding,' Olivia had said, giving them the best of hugs. 'It's yours.'

'I'll be your wedding photographer,' said Hoppy, who had a Nikon and loved to use it.

'I'll make the pies,' said Olivia, who had learned pie baking from a former housekeeper and was proud to call it her specialty.

'Cherry!' Dooley had said, about to throw up from stress.

That had gone so much better than expected; she felt really grateful and later wrote them a long letter.

But she and Dooley still had to tell Father Tim. Everyone knew he hoped to marry them in the Lord's Chapel rose garden that he and Harley and Dooley's brother, Sammy, recovered from ruin. Everyone knew he had trained the Seven Sisters vines to climb in a really special way on the arch, just for this day.

Lord's Chapel was where she and Dooley were confirmed and baptized, and where Father Tim and Cynthia and Hoppy and Olivia were married. It was the family church.

She and Dooley had gone one evening to the yellow house. 'Give me a sign,' Dooley said, 'like when you think it's a good time.'

There is no good time for this, she thought.

Cynthia had made spaghetti, and later they all sat by the fire in the study. Dooley jiggled his leg a lot and was finally able to say it. 'We just want to get married at home, Dad. At Meadowgate. With family and a few friends.'

Father Tim had blinked and there was a long pause as if he was trying to absorb what he heard.

She looked at Dooley, who was miserable. They had tried so hard to do everything right. Like taking seriously the statistics of a high divorce rate in vet school and the rigor of the courses. They had gone through the awful hunger and frustration of being apart, and the endless road trips that connected the dots between Atlanta and Athens and Mitford and Chapel Hill and Farmer and NC State, where Dooley transferred after college. They had gone through four speeding tickets in as many years, two each, not to mention a huge stack of CDs. And now they both wanted to just be at home, please, God—at Meadowgate with family.

Father Tim had smiled then, and nodded. 'Good,' he said like he really, really meant it. 'Getting married at home is good.'

She had also written them a long letter.

So no Vera or Oscar or hair bound up in a chignon. She knew all about those beautiful, seductive things; she had spent years looking at dresses and hairstyles and being a bridesmaid at glamorous weddings. Then for some reason she never expected, none of that mattered anymore. She had done it in her head over and over—the shoes, the jewelry, the music; she had walked down the aisle a thousand times and saw heads turning and heard the little gasps of approval. She felt a new kind of joy in knowing that she and Dooley would have something more wonderful than the grand wedding, the awesome honeymoon, the lingerie as ephemeral as mist.

'We could even have a barefoot wedding,' she said to Dooley.

'Wait'll y'uns step on a bee,' said Harley. 'Or one of them black snakes. That'll cure y' of barefooted, I can tell y' that.'

She and Dooley had dug deep to wait through the last years of college and vet school. How would she direct herself while he focused on academics? Her art instructors had been crazy about her portfolio; they said she could go anywhere and do anything. So she pursued jobs in publishing, in advertising, and then in design, but wherever she applied, it was 'the economy.' Here, there, everywhere, the economy.

While Dooley was on a totally defined path, she was constantly trying to figure things out in a wandering sort of way. She resisted, without really understanding why, Olivia's generous offer to underwrite a graduate program in art and design at Pratt, which anybody in their right mind would go for if they could get accepted. She adored Hoppy and Olivia, who had given her everything, including their name and their amazing love, but the answer was no, and so there she went again, wandering like an Israelite.

What saved her in these final couple of years was teaching art to children at a nonprofit in Chapel Hill, where she moved to be near Dooley. She had learned more from her students than she could ever teach. It had been, in some ways, the time of her life, and she had loved each of them fiercely.

Perhaps she would teach again one day. But what she wanted now was to work with Dooley in the clinic. Though it was an established vet practice of thirty-five years, the changeover would be big and how they handled it would be important. She would be there for Dooley completely.

Dooley stopped and wiped the perspiration pearling on his forehead. 'You've been workin' really hard. You and Cynthia both. Thanks for everything. I want you to know we appreciate it.'

'Thank you,' he said, 'for the chance to do it. We're having a good time.'

Herding Dooley's new cattle into the pasture a couple of weeks ago had been the hoot of the month. They were a start-up herd of five heifers with the self-determination of a vestry. It had taken a village to get them off the truck and through the open cattle gate. The hauler had left more room than needed between the trailer doors and the gate, so there went Willie and Harley, racing to head one off from the barn, and there was Lily brandishing her apron like a matador as another trotted toward the corncrib. He had stood by the trailer like a bump on a log, waiting for directions from Dooley.

'I was no help,' he said later of receiving no directions.

'I didn't want you running around like that.'

'Because I'm old?'

'Not *old*. But well, you know . . .'

He did know. He'd be into the double sevens at the end of June. Knees stiff, harder to keep the weight down, the occasional diabetic flare-up. Worse, he hadn't run seriously for nearly a year, something he hadn't confided to his doctor, who ran twenty miles, three days a week.

They worked for a time, silent. The buzzing of flies, a vagrant bee, the scent of grasses they were trampling.

Nobody was talking about the honeymoon. All he and Cynthia knew was that Hoppy and Olivia had offered something exotic, Hawaii or the Caymans, he couldn't remember, and according to Cynthia, the offer had been 'gently declined.'

'So. Any honeymoon plans yet?'

'See that house in the grove? That window over the front porch? That's it.'

'Aha. If you change your mind, you know we'll do anything we can. We'll help sit the farm, give a hand to Willie and Harley.' He and Cynthia had sat the farm for the Owens a few years back and managed pretty well.

'What would you do if Choo-Choo and th' girls got out?'

'I'd do whatever Willie and Harley were doing.'

Dooley laughed. Things were okay. What he'd said earlier about children had been forgotten.

'Hammer an' staples,' said the fence doctor.

Ha! Something he could absolutely recognize.

'Sammy's pumped about coming to the wedding,' said Dooley. 'He texted me last night.'

Sammy. Almost twenty-two, now, with a manager, dental veneers, and a hot name on the pro pool circuit. He had hoped to adopt Dooley's brother a few years back, but Sammy Barlowe didn't want to be adopted. 'My daddy made Barlowe a bad name,' Sammy said. 'I'm goin' to make Barlowe a good name.'

He had loved Sammy as well as he knew how. But it was Father Brad, the then-new hire at Lord's Chapel, who had stepped up to the plate and worked wonders. Thank God for Father Brad's boot camp. He would take the camp himself if he weren't so . . . along in years? Aged out? What was the language to be learned for being old?

Dooley worked for a time, silent, squinting, then stood back and viewed the repair. 'Done. That's it. We can pack up and go in.'

He was more than proud of his son's vet school credentials and his wedding coming up and his bull coming in.

Youth wasn't entirely wasted on the young. But he was sobered, too—by the big responsibilities that lay ahead. It was no dream anymore, it was the real deal.

'I'm in over my head, Dad. I look at you—always so patient. I can never be patient like you.'

'I don't know that I'm so patient. Ambrose Bierce called patience a minor form of despair, disguised as a virtue.' He had always liked that.

'You goin' to cry at my wedding?'

'I'm not planning to cry. I'll leave that to the women.'

Dooley grinned, wiped his hands on a rag. 'I cried at your wedding.'

'You did?' What a wonderful thing to know. 'So, okay. I'll cry at yours.'

They had a laugh. He put his arm around his boy, slapped him on the back.

'I love you,' he said.

She sat on the side of her bed and stared at the painting without seeing it.

It was easy now to forget the fights and the tears, but still hard to forget the devastating disappointment that came nearly a year ago and the grieving that followed. She had wondered if they could survive that, but they did, because there was love they didn't even know they had till then. A raw new strength was born from that grief, and for the first time they both understood that no matter what, they could do this.

So the waiting had been a good thing, like a huge investment sufficient to pay out over a lifetime. Most important, the waiting had been worth it because she had lost the fear of surrendering her heart. For years she had believed her strong will could be enough to make their relationship work. At one point she decided her courage could be enough. And during one of her crazier phases she tried to believe that just being pretty, as some said she was, could be enough.

But none of that was enough for the great journey they would be taking. She came to know this during his second year at vet school, after a long week of prayer and loneliness and weeping. She had surrendered her heart once before, as a kid, when Preacher Greer brought revival to the Creek. She had jumped down from the tree limb and Preacher Greer had prayed for her and she was warm for the first time in her life. To think that she must again surrender the core of her being was too much. Surely it was more than was needed to get by.

He had come home to Mitford that last weekend of October—documented in her Dooley book for three long pages—and with an ease unlike any she might imagine, she had at last opened her heart to him completely.

It was every prayer answered, every benediction composed into one.

She remembered his weekend smell of a burger on the highway and his shampoo and his favorite jacket with the top button missing, all that, and his hands cold from the October wind. She had held him, unguarded and certain, and he looked at her and she knew that he understood. Dooley really got stuff that didn't come with words.

Words! For days she had wanted to write a special word in the Dooley book, but things had been so crazy. She cleaned her brushes and went to the shelf and took down the once-blank book and let it fall open of its own accord. Some days it fell open to the really good times. Now it fell open to the other times.

Oct 19~ He called last night and said he was sorry. We are always sorry about something with each other; then we have to go back to school before we finish working things out. This is incredibly hard. Sometimes I don't want to do it anymore and he says he doesn't either. But we can't stop. I can't stop loving him.

Oct 22~ I painted all day yesterday. Drove to the country and had no idea where I was going. Found a farm and climbed over the fence and set up my easel in the field. D doesn't understand how solitude is the only way to get my work done~ he is always 'up and doing with a heart for any fate,' according to Fr Tim. But people say we are so much alike~ both of us with scary childhoods, both adopted by people who gave us everything, both working hard in school to prove whatever. But we aren't alike at all. It was our experiences that were alike. I am quick flame, he is slow-burning ember. *Or maybe it's the other way around. Our counselor who has a woodstove says any good fire is both.*

Oct 25~ D almost never tells me what he's thinking. It's like when we're together I'm jumping into a river with no idea which way the current is moving.

The counselor Olivia gives us lives near the grounds at school. But unless D comes here, we have to do the sessions on the phone like a conference call. D definitely does not like to do this, but we know it is helping. I can't really think about anything right now without crying, I didn't cry for years because I couldn't. Olivia says crying is good for nearly everything and she should know since she had a heart transplant before she and Hoppy were married. She says if it hadn't been for Hoppy diagnosing the issue and getting her to Boston, she would not be here to cry ever again.

Nov 6~ It was this date ten years ago when I was legally adopted by Olivia and Hoppy and since I never had a middle name the attorneys said if I wanted one this would be a good time so I took Harper. That will be your last name, they said, do you also want it for a middle name? And I said yes.

I could not imagine O and H would keep me forever and if anything happened I would always have this special name. I thought they pitied me~ a poor Creek kid in a mashed-up hat with stringy hair and dirty clothes.

They kept loving me but I had a terrible fear of loving

17

them back. I did everything I could to keep from loving them back.

It was totally exhausting for all of us. I could see it in Hoppy's face where I also saw patients dying and his heart condition that he wouldn't confront and the years of lost sleep and Olivia's drained look when we tried to talk. All of it probably caused by regret that they had taken me in. All I knew is that I did not deserve to be loved~ it was their own fault for trying to do the impossible. I wanted them to just leave me alone because they didn't deserve to suffer because I couldn't love them back.

And then the year I studied in France and painted and they came to see me and somehow~ I honestly think it was the way the light moved over the lavender fields~ my heart was very full for them and grateful and I was able to say to the concierge, These are my parents!

I felt a stone lift off my heart. After that I said it to everyone~ my parents, my parents!

Thank you, God, for helping us through hard times. They are my mom and dad forever.

Maybe the 20th~ D and I talk a lot about living at Meadowgate. It has felt like home to us for years. If we ever marry~ it is scary to write that word!~ I want to stay at home. But I never tell anyone I would like to stay home. What's so wrong with that anyway? Beth dreams of a big job at Goldman Sachs and Laurel wants to design cars. Cars! And she doesn't want children. She says no way.

D and I agree that four would be perfect. He helped raise his four sibs when he was little. He was ten years old and feeding them out of cans and then they all got scattered to the wind and all but Pooh were lost for years. We will never let scattering happen.

Nov 28~ Dooley wants to feel safe with me, but he can't. And I don't really feel safe with him because I don't know where this is going. Beth says that knowing where a relationship is going doesn't solve everything.

She let the journal lie open in her lap. She shouldn't be reading these entries when there were so many happy ones. But the old stuff was good, too—it was a reminder.

She was aware of another reminder—the pain that was so familiar she sometimes forgot it. She reached for the pills she kept in a box on a shelf with the old Britannicas, and swallowed one with a glass of water from their well.

It was her night to make supper happen and she'd hardly given it a thought. Meadowgate was a total commune right now. When the Owens moved out a month ago, she and Father Tim and Cynthia and Harley piled their belongings into three vehicles and moved into this rambling old house, where everybody immediately went to work making things ready for June fourteenth, for the beginning of another life.

Father Tim and Cynthia would move home to Mitford the night of the wedding, but Harley would stay on, helping with farm chores and general improvements and living in Rebecca Jane's old room with the princess canopy bed. Harley had been her true family when she lived at the Creek; he had been the best place to run when she needed to hide from her father. Not only had Harley protected her when he could, he had encouraged her passion for books and learning. Harley was the best, and now she would take care of him, which was great with Dooley since he also considered Harley 'blood.'

She loved having family around, including Willie, who had his own little house on the place. He had been the main hand at Meadowgate for years and was always in and out with his weather predictions. Sometimes Blake Eddistoe, Hal's vet tech who would stay on in the practice, stuck around for supper, and sometimes Rebecca Jane Owen, almost sixteen and still crazy about Dooley, would come over with her mom and dad, and there was Lily Flower, who cleaned two days a week and was such a fun nutcase and worked harder than anybody and sometimes had supper with them and washed up after.

Okay. Boiled red potatoes with chives and butter. A salad. And roast chicken with rosemary from the garden. Not two chickens, but three. Enough to make great sandwiches for tomorrow's lunch and soup after.

She paged forward to a blank sheet in the Dooley book, took a deep breath, and wrote the word: *Cherish.*

She did not date the entry.

She returned the book to the shelf and hurried to the west-facing windows of the attic studio. In the far corner of the fence line, she saw them. Dooley and Father Tim were specks as they climbed into the truck.

'Dooley!' Her breath formed a small vapor on the glass.

She lifted her hand and waved, though she knew he couldn't see her.

'I've been meaning to ask,' he told Cynthia as he changed clothes for supper. 'What do you wear to a potluck wedding?' He couldn't just float around all day with his vestments flapping in the breeze.

'Very casual.'

'A knit shirt?'

'I don't know about a knit shirt,' she said. 'Maybe too much of a golfer look.'

'So, a white dress shirt, maybe? Without the starch?'

'How about your blue stripe or your blue check? And khakis, I think.'

Khakis. This would be a first. Back in the day, seersucker suits had been de rigueur for Mississippi summer weddings.

'And socks with your loafers,' she said. 'Loafers without socks is sort of a good-old-boy look, someone said.'

He ran a comb through what was left of his hair. 'I'm a pretty good old boy.'

'The chickens will be done in twenty minutes,' said Lace. 'If you could please take them out?'

'Will do.' Cynthia was putting potatoes on to boil.

'I just need to run up to Heaven. Back in a flash.'

'I know the feeling. Take your time.'

She did run. All the way to the top of the house to the room Cynthia had called Heaven and claimed as her art studio while living at Meadowgate years ago.

Right there! On just this apple at just this spot, this one simple thing. She brushed in a rough semblance of the *Coccinella septempunctata* and stood back. *Yes.* Cecil Kennedy would be crazy about it if he weren't dead as anything. She wished she could work on it right now, but no way; maybe tomorrow. This painting would rock.

Dooley had come in; she could hear his voice all the way from the kitchen.

She cleaned her brush and, inhaling the aromas rising from the oven, ran down the stairs. Yes, yes, yes, yes, yes, yes, yes . . .

She was starved and he would be, too.

Two

He had never been to a wedding except the one for his two cousins in Kentucky when he was still haulin' liquor. They were cousins by marriage, not by blood, so no chance of any funny business happenin' to their young'uns.

'What am I gon' wear?' said Harley.

'Your teeth, for sure,' said Lace. 'And a clean shirt and khakis. I'll lay it all out on your bed.'

That dadgum bed. He was mighty thankful to have a bed an' wouldn't complain, but it was criminal for a grown man to be sleepin' in a pink bedstead with a ruffled thingamajig on top.

'Man,' said Dooley.

She put her hand on his leg—her signal for him to stop jiggling, as she called it.

The house was quiet now, people sleeping, a bit of light from Father Tim and Cynthia's window—Father Tim would be reading in the room that he and Cynthia would turn over to the newlyweds after the wedding. And Harley, Harley would be snoring downstairs in Rebecca Jane's left-behind princess bed, and Willie would be having his midnight snack of cornbread and milk in the little house with walls covered by vintage calendars from the tractor supply, and over at Hilltop, Hal and Marge and Rebecca Jane would be sleeping in rooms still smelling of fresh paint . . .

It was strangely calming to know where everyone was, including Bowser, Bo, Buck, and Bonemeal, the four old farm dogs slung up on the porch at their feet. When Hal and Marge moved to the hill, they had taken five canines, but four had come back and wouldn't go again. They had seen the new place and didn't care for it; this was home.

It had been a long day for Dooley, for everyone at Meadowgate. The clinic closed on Saturdays at noon, but he'd gone in at seven-thirty and looked at the books and rearranged his office and cussed his copier and had a meeting with Hal and Blake and greeted everybody who came through the door. He'd given shots to the heifers, improved the way the south well had been closed up, and checked out the barn loft for hay storage.

'Five rotten timbers,' he said. 'Could be worse.' He closed his eyes and leaned back against the cushion of the porch glider. 'All the waiting we did to get here, and we thought that was hard.' He exhaled. 'Dreams are a lot of work.'

And she didn't have a dress yet and there were the rentals to be preordered from Holding, who had to order them from Charlotte—tables, chairs, tablecloths, napkins, plates, flatware, glasses. And lanterns to be found for the tables, probably at the co-op—Cynthia would help her paint them—and the invitations waiting to be addressed and this time she would say yes to Olivia, who had volunteered to arrange the flowers, and of course she and Lily would soon be getting on with the rosemary bread they would bake and freeze, four loaves per table, plus cheese wafers . . .

'Are we crazy?'

Dooley laughed. 'Still crazy after all these years.'

'How many years? I bet you can't remember.'

'The first time I saw you,' he said, 'you were twelve going on twenty-four.' His eyes were closed and he was grinning.

'And you were thirteen. You were wearing a blue shirt with a button-down collar.' She didn't remember ever seeing a button-down collar before; she was jealous of his shirt.

He had been a total snot, but she'd never seen anybody as cute and for some reason it made her mad that he was that cute and getting away with it.

'I can't believe it,' he said.

'What?'

'The thing about time. How it flies. I thought only old people thought that.'

'What I can't believe is, I'm marrying the bratty derp who stole my hat.'

He laughed. 'And I'm marrying that weird Creek kid who punched me for stealing it. That's really unbelievable.'

Out there were stars and planets and the dark procession of cedars along the fence line.

He wondered how often they had sat on this wicker glider, talking against the night, against the morning when he or she or both would have to get in the car and drive like a rock star and clock in somewhere else. Hal and Marge had gladly conveyed the beat-up porch furniture with the sale, along with a lot of other stuff he and Lace had grown accustomed to. He liked familiar things, things that had been worn in by good people, people he could trust. This afternoon he had bought back the truck he sold his dad a few years ago. He felt safe in that truck, it was worn in just right.

This was her favorite time. Crickets and stars and the person she would spend the rest of her life with. 'The pool table is coming out Monday,' she said.

'Where are you putting it?' he said.

'In the library. Cynthia says she'll miss having it fill up their entire dining room. Harley will bring the library chairs to my studio, and speaking of chairs, I think we should rent the wood finish, not white. Four hundred and twenty dollars for chairs for the ceremony and supper.'

'Do it,' he said. 'It's your day.'

'Our day.'

'I've been thinking about the tent. A guy at school says a tent rental for fifty people at a sit-down would cost twelve hundred bucks, maybe more. Not in our budget.'

'But if it rains . . .' Willie pretty much promised rain, a prediction that had made him briefly unpopular.

'The barn. Tables for ten, end to end, to make one long table down the center aisle. If it rains, the shed will keep it from blowing into the barn.'

'I love that. It's perfect.'

'So we could put the food tables in the grain room, sans mice; we'll take the door off. And muck out the stalls.'

'The stalls should be easy; the girls haven't used them much. I can do that.'

'Brides don't muck out stalls,' he said.

'But I like doing it, remember? I used to do it when Hal and Marge had horses. It's very grounding.'

He gave her a thoughtful look. 'You're amazing.'

She didn't feel amazing; she felt worn, somehow. 'So what about a tent for the ceremony? We need a tent. We can't just sit out in the open. I mean, we could, but if . . .'

'If rain's predicted, we could do the ceremony on the front porch. We can get fifty chairs on the porch. Ten rows five chairs wide. I measured, we can do it.'

Why remind him that rain hardly ever falls straight down, it falls at a slant? But she was stressing too much about these things, she needed to lighten up.

'It will be a great day,' he said. 'Come rain or come shine.'

'That's an old-fashioned thing my mother used to say before she got sick. Like, she'd scrub the floor tomorrow, come rain or come shine.'

'My granpa used to say it, too.'

'I never hear you talk about him.'

'He was good to me. He saved my life by dumping me on Dad. If he hadn't done that, we probably wouldn't be sitting here tonight. Granpa was too old to do much, and then he was too sick, but he did the best he could while I was with him. He always said, I'm gon' take care of you, boy, come rain or come shine.'

He'd never thanked his granpa, Russell Jacks, who was sexton at Lord's Chapel for a lot of years. He'd been too young and too confused to think about thanking. Obviously, it was too late—or maybe, as some liked to think, it was never too late.

'I've been coming out here since I was eleven years old,' he said. 'Why am I just now getting it in my head that there's a lot of work on this place? Nothing ever seemed like work before.'

'You see the work now because it's yours.'

'Ours,' he said.

'Imagine those funny girls with their heads sticking over the stall doors while we're having potluck.' She laughed, a sudden thing, like a cloudburst. It made her feel herself again.

'We need to keep them out of the barn till hot weather, when they'll need the stalls for shade. By the way, keep reminding everybody to shut the big gate after they feed up.'

'I will.'

'We haven't had to close it in a couple of years, so it's easy to forget. The clinic sign will be ready for us to bring home after graduation. It looks great.'

Everyone who drove the Farmer road would see it hanging on its post in a bed of red and yellow zinnias.

'I'll be back on it in two weeks.' He wouldn't come home next weekend; he would spend it packing up his stuff, saying goodbye, doing a little partying with friends. Then the gown, the crazy hat, the whole nine yards, and immediately after, he was bustin' out of the academic world.

'Doctor Kavanagh!' She looked at him with a kind of wonder. 'I can't believe it.'

He thought there was an awful lot they couldn't believe these days.

'Harley, Hal, Marge, and Rebecca Jane, who still adores you, will all be there,' she said. 'They're coming in Hal's van.'

'Hal's van smells like old dogs.'

'They'll drive with the windows down.'

They laughed a little, holding each other in this moment that wouldn't come again.

'Hoppy and Olivia are driving up from Charleston, where Hoppy is making a speech, and I'll come with your parents.'

He jiggled his leg; there was too much going on.

'It would be perfect if all your sibs could come to the wedding,' she said. 'I know Kenny and Julie can't afford to fly from Oregon and bring the kids, but if I could sell . . .'

'It's okay. They'll come later. Kenny has a great job doing what he loves, and it's not the best time for him to leave, anyway.'

Something about the bridge Kenny was working on and the government funding going sour.

'Anyway, all the others will be here,' he said. 'I talked to Sammy today. He's in Minnesota. A trick shot competition.'

She could see Sammy hunkered over the pool table with his ponytail and the burning look he had when blowing everybody out of the water. And now he was on cable TV, and winning trophies and making money.

She wished her wedding dress would present itself in her mind as clearly as the image of Sammy breaking a rack. Something soft. Ankle-length. Simple but amazing. That's all she knew. And the Seven Sisters roses in a bouquet with rosemary, and a satin ribbon the color of Jersey cream . . .

Rebecca Jane was up for catching the bouquet. 'Throw it to *me!*' she had begged. 'It's okay that I'll be a nun and never, ever get married.'

She took his hand and felt the beating of his pulse. They hadn't really talked about his mother coming to the wedding, and how Sammy would feel about it. Sammy hadn't seen her since he was six years old—Pauline had abandoned all but one of her five children when they were really young. But Pauline had changed, of course. Everything about her life had changed, and maybe the wedding would work some miracle for Sammy and his mother. Everybody was praying for that.

'Inviting her is the right thing to do,' Dooley had said. 'Sammy and Mama—that's their deal, not mine. So there'll be some tension. There's always some tension at weddings, right?' He had been a groomsman more than a few times.

A heifer bawled from the pasture and was quiet again. He

wanted to crash on the bed in his room next to the porch and sleep for weeks. But he couldn't leave her, not yet—their whole history had been about leaving.

'I wanted to tell him today,' he said. 'He mentioned something about . . .'

'Children.'

'Yes.'

'I can't be with you when you tell him. I'll cry and I don't want to.'

'It's okay,' he said. 'I'll do it.'

'But I can tell Cynthia. Hoppy and Olivia and Hal and Marge have known it for so long, I've felt guilty about not telling your parents.' Dooley had wanted to do it sooner, but couldn't.

'So before I leave in the morning,' he said. 'It's really bothering me, I've got to do it.'

'I'll talk to Cynthia while you talk to him. But we can't say anything to anybody about Jack Tyler.'

'I know. It's too soon.'

He needed to say how much she meant to him, how much he loved and wanted her, but he couldn't manage to say anything right now. Professor Morgan had called him 'a lad of few words.' That wasn't true. There were words spilling around in him all the time. Too many words. His problem was organizing them.

He had held himself away from her for years until that Christmas at Meadowgate. It had snowed and they had gone out in it with Bowser and Bonemeal and a sled and she was wearing the jacket with the hood and the snow was coming down very fast and he couldn't believe how beautiful she was, so beautiful in some new way that he felt he didn't deserve such beauty, it was beyond him. He was struck by the sudden understanding that he could lose her by not loving her enough.

He had gripped her hand and they moved on. He was carrying a weight he couldn't identify—a heaviness that must be given up.

They had stopped to look over their tracks and across to the farmhouse with its vine of smoke from the kitchen chimney. Something shifted in him then, and he knew without thinking what was about to happen. He was terrified, but didn't look down. He leaped from one bank of the chasm to the other—and she received him with a tenderness he couldn't name. He was safe; he was home.

He drew her closer, felt the beating of her heart. A lot of times their hearts beat in different rhythms, but tonight they beat together, a rare thing that had never happened with anyone else.

After breakfast he walked out with his dad and they sat on a bench under the barn shed.

There would be no children for them; they had known it for quite a while. They had processed this truth in several different ways, which took time and emotional energy, and they hadn't really been ready to talk about it.

Lace had been diagnosed with adhesive disease, caused by infections due to rupture in the abdominal cavity. The problem, which was almost constantly painful, couldn't be detected by CAT scans or MRI images and for years had been treated as irritable bowel syndrome.

Her father had kicked her twice in the abdomen. 'The first time,' said Dooley, 'she was seven years old. The second time, she was ten.' She had been frightened by the menstrual blood and the terrible yelling of her father, and her mother hiding beneath the bedcovers.

He said all this as best he could without flying into a rage or breaking down. He had broken down once in a KFC drive-through, once when talking to a professor, and more than a few times with Lace.

Dooley stood and caught his breath. All the telling had been done now; it was nobody else's business. He felt some of the fury and sorrow lift off and saw that his dad was weeping, and in a gesture in which he felt like the parent, he put his arm around his dad's shoulders and promised himself this would be the last time he would mourn what could not be changed.

Three

The smells of Lily's breakfast wafted his way.

He finagled his morning insulin shot and stood by the bedroom window, buttoning his shirt. Ha! There was Harley getting out of an older-model car with a ski rack.

'I just saw Harley coming in,' he told Willie.

'Been over at Jake's for a sausage biscuit. With th' woman he met when he hitched home from th' tire store.' Willie set a hatful of eggs on the kitchen counter.

'He looks mighty jaunty.'

'They went for a ride last evenin'.' Willie gave him a look.

As a parson, he was accustomed to knowing what was going on with people. He was completely in the dark about this. 'How old is this person?'

'Says she's th' same age as him.'

'Must not be her ski rack, then.'

'Nossir, she don't ski, but says a rack makes 'er feel young.'

'That's one way,' he said.

He walked to the barn with Harley, who would be foreman on the removal and replacement of the barn's rotten floorboards.

'She wants me to go t' Las Vegas,' said Harley. 'She'll do th' drivin'.'

'Las Vegas, *Nevada?*'

'You can see th' pyramids, she says, I always wanted to see th' pyramids, an' you can ride in a boat on a river inside a buildin'.'

'No way,' he said.

'Yessir, she's been there in person.'

He opened the barn door; Daisy, LuLu, and Pete came running to the cat bowls.

'When is this to take place?'

'I ain't said nothin' to Dooley yet. Sometime after th' weddin', like ever'thing else.'

'You really want to go to Las Vegas?'

'Life is short,' said Harley. 'God is good. An' th' best things in life are free.'

He had never heard talk like this from Harley Welch.

'Las Vegas is not free. I know that much.'

'I've got a little money saved back. A good bit, t' tell th' truth.'

He scooped dry food into the bowls.

'Does this person know that?'

'I told her right down to th' penny, an' Amber, she says she's got a good bit saved back her ownself.'

He was no mother hen, but he didn't like the sound of this.

'Maybe we should invite her over for . . . I don't know . . . a glass of tea?'

'Why?' said Cynthia.

'To check her out.'

'Harley is a grown man.'

'But Las *Vegas*? With a woman driving a *ski rack*?' Where were his wife's *instincts*?

'I don't believe Harley would actually stray that far from home. Anyway, I thought he was smitten with Miss Pringle.'

'Harley was smitten with Miss Pringle when he was with Miss Pringle, and now he's with this Amber person.' He remembered the book that came out in the forties, which Tommy Noles found in his mother's apron drawer. He had been interested in the map of London in the frontispiece until Tommy showed him what was what.

His wife gave him a smile. 'She has a roofing business.'

'A what?'

'A roofing business.'

'Cynthia. Listen to me. This cannot go on. This ski person is not Harley's type. A roofing business!'

'Roofing can be very lucrative.'

Sometimes it was hard being married to an open-minded woman.

He would ask Lily, who catered the Wesley mayor's annual shindig and knew everybody in these coves and hollers.

'Amber,' he said.

'What's her last name?'

'I have no idea, I thought the first name would be enough to . . . you don't know her?'

'I do not know anybody named Amber in the roofin' business.'

'So who do you know in the roofing business?'

'Tim Bolick. Randy Chase. Billy Upton. Charlie Knight. That's it.'

'Can you call around and see if they know anything about this person?'

She gave him a squinty look.

'Early-model Toyota hatchback,' he said. 'White. Ski rack.'

'I never said she was a roofer, I said she's a hoofer.'

He was stunned. 'A hoofer?'

'A dancer,' said Harley, grinning.

He wished Harley would put his teeth in, he had gotten used to seeing them. 'A dancer?'

'Yessir.'

'At her age?'

'She says look at Tina Turner.'

He literally raced to find his wife, who was sitting on the floor in the front hall, painting baseboards.

'Remember,' she said, 'that you swore to never get involved again in somebody's romance.'

'Did I say that?'

'When Shirlene and Omer . . .'

'But that turned out great. They're happily married!'

'Correct. But you said you would completely quit meddling in people's romances.'

So his wife was confirming that it was a romance. It was official.

'Harley says she's not a roofer. She's a hoofer.'

'A hoofer?'

'A dancer.'

'An exotic dancer?'

'I have no idea,' he said.

Who would stop this craziness? Why was he always the one to worry about things?

His wife looked up at him, puzzled. 'But where in heaven's name would she *hoof* in these mountains? I mean, really, honey. Think about it.'

'Maybe she doesn't live here, she's just passing through.' More reason to be concerned.

Getting no help from his wife, he went to see Lace in her attic studio. There had been zero chance to speak with her since his talk with Dooley yesterday morning, and now wouldn't be a good time. People could not write sermons or paint paintings or accomplish much of anything with people knocking on the door, but this was *life* and so be it.

'It's you!' said Lace, obviously pleased.

He made his apologies. 'This Amber person is not a roofer, she's a hoofer.'

'I know.' She wiped her knife with a rag. 'He seems so happy about her. But of course he can't go to Las Vegas and let her spend his money.'

Thanks be to God, there was someone in this household with a rational world view.

'Praying for you,' he said, awkward. 'I'm sorry.' Worse than sorry, he and Cynthia were grieved, but this wasn't the time.

'It's okay,' she said, hoping to make him feel better. It wasn't really okay, but maybe it would be, could be . . .

'Should we call Miss Pringle? Invite her out for . . . a little visit?'

Lace laid the knife in the easel tray. 'I think it's too late for Miss Pringle.'

Too late for Miss Pringle!

Down he went to the kitchen, where Lily was scrubbing the bare pine floor.

'What did you hear from your roofers?'

'Nothin'. They're all workin', is my guess. It's good roofin' weather.'

'It's just as well. This Amber person is not a roofer, she's a hoofer.'

'A what?'

'A hoofer. A dancer.'

'Oh, boy,' said Lily. 'This train is movin'. He's got a date this evenin'. He asked me if I thought he was too old to call it a date.'

'I was pretty old,' he said, 'and I called it a date.'

'Well, there you go. You want a glass of tea?'

'No, thanks.'

He looked at the current job list pushpinned to the cork-board beside the back door.

Weed ALL borders once weekly prior to 14th

Measure barn aisle to the inch TODAY

It was clear that this list had been written by his wife, who was fond of capital letters and telling people what to do.

Work ROTTED barn dirt into kitchen garden

Weed-eat chicken run TODAY and AGAIN June 13

Order SIX flats white impatiens at co-op for pickup May 14

Mark your calendar to plant impatiens either side barn
*   door on May 15—remember to WATER after planting*

Pick up signpost and green paint next Tuesday at co-op

Day before wedding, use pooper scooper around main house
*   AND path to barn*

Remember to CHECK FINISHED PROJECTS OFF
*   THIS LIST*

'Are you okay?' said Lily.

'I am.'

'You don't look it.'

'Thank you,' he said.

'It's th' red Agnes!' She peered out the window to the pasture. 'They are so cute.'

'*Angus*,' he said for the fourth or fifth time.

'Right,' she said.

Seven-thirty. Cloudy. Cool.

Before entangling himself in the day's fray, he walked to the corncrib and turned right, glad to be wearing a warm jacket.

The cat Sammy brought home to them a few years ago followed like a pup. He and Cynthia missed Violet, who lived on in the numerous books Cynthia had written and illustrated about her white cat. Now here was this little guy, white with a black ear, and ever full of cheer and affection. Truman was up for country living, though oddly disdainful of mice and eager for his daily handout in the kitchen.

He opened the gate to a small cemetery plot overhung by the branches of two lindens and sat on the bench.

'Lord.' He crossed himself and spoke aloud to that place beyond the fence, the fields, the blue bowl of the April sky.

'I'm here for the sundered nest, the families broken apart by anger, disappointment, violence, neglect. Thank you in advance for your mercy and grace upon Pauline, Dooley, Kenny, Sammy, Pooh, Jessie, and all those you have associated with their lives and with their suffering. You told the farmer Joel that you would restore unto him the days the locusts had eaten. For the Barlowes and for all such families, Lord, we thank you for restoring those days to each and every one.'

Truman leaped onto the bench, purred beneath the mortal warmth of his hand.

'Through Christ our Lord,' he said, looking across to the stone marker.

He had ordered the stone, highly deserving of the lapidary treatment, engraved with an epitaph written in 1808 by John Hobhouse.

BARNABAS

. . . WHO POSSESSED BEAUTY
WITHOUT VANITY

STRENGTH WITHOUT INSOLENCE

COURAGE WITHOUT FEROCITY

AND ALL THE VIRTUES OF MAN
WITHOUT HIS VICES

Four years ago, Barnabas had passed as he, Timothy, wished to pass—in his sleep.

Fourteen years of companionship, understanding, devotion, and a fine regard for Holy Scripture. There would never be another like Barnabas, nor would he ever have another of any breed or kind. His good dog, with all the virtues of man without his vices, had been dog enough for a lifetime.

The men were given bag lunches—'to eat under a tree' was Lace's directive.

'Which tree?' said Harley.

Hal joined them while Blake wormed a litter of beagle pups and gave a health check to the Sweeneys' goat.

They chose the maple tree at the head of the clinic driveway and settled down with four dogs, Truman, and the barn cats up for a handout.

They ate their BLTs and drank their tea with appetite. Thereby consoled for their labors, they fetched out the quarters.

'Here's your toss line,' said Willie. He took a wad of string from his pocket and laid a length of it on the asphalt drive at a point roughly ten or twelve feet from the lunch crowd.

Harley had a pocketful of quarters. Willie confessed to having seven. As for himself, he was carrying ten or twelve. Hal preferred to take a quick nap. The player who tossed his coin closest to the line would win all the quarters.

He had a fleeting realization, a small epiphany, that every simple thing—a game of Toss to the Line, a bottle of tea after a morning's labor, the laughter of Cynthia and Lace and Olivia and Marge and Lily from the kitchen—all seemed especially holy and good.

Weather for June fourteenth was a chewy, and occasionally sore, subject. In the blessing over dinner, for which they all traditionally held hands, he included yet another petition for good weather for the Big Knot.

Willie weighed in with a decidedly arcane morsel of information. 'Up in Virginia, I hear they bury a bottle of bourbon a week before th' weddin'.'

'So?' he said.

'To make sure th' weather's nice for th' big day.'

'Who gits to bury it?' said Harley.

'Who gits to dig it up?' said Lily. 'That is th' question.'

The notion of whether there would be enough food was another topic. Shouldn't there be some kind of organization in this potluck deal? Shouldn't somebody get on the phone and call the guest list? What if they ended up with too many deviled eggs?

'There is no such thing as too many deviled eggs,' said Cynthia.

Or what if they all came with fried chicken?

'Fine by me,' said Hal, who claimed that's what he would order for his last meal on earth, given the opportunity.

Potluck Paranoia had definitely set in. It rocketed past The Dress and rose quickly to number two in popularity after Weather Anxiety.

He helped Lily wash up.

'Tim Bolick called me back,' she said.

'Who's Tim Bolick?'

'One of th' roofers you asked me to call. He knows Amber di . . . let's see . . . di Domenico.'

He sat down, still holding the dish towel. 'What does she do for a living?'

'He didn't know. He patched her roof. It was leakin' around th' chimney. He said she's got a good many cats.'

'Cats?'

'She takes in rescue cats. Maybe thirty or so, he said.'

He didn't know where to go with this.

'Nice?' he said.

'Th' cats?'

'Her. She.'

'Tim says she's real nice. A little old, he said.'

He knew about being nice and old.

He couldn't sleep. Eleven p.m., and not a wink after a hard day at the list. Hammering away all morning, weed-eating in the afternoon. He was not a fan of weed-eating.

And no way was Harley's Amber escapade keeping him

awake. His antsy sleeplessness happened about twice a week, whether at home or abroad.

With his wife snoring like a teenager, he was up and moving around—opening a window, listening to the night, closing the window. He walked to the chest of drawers and turned on the lamp and looked at the cross propped against it. Sammy had given it to him the Christmas that Lace and Dooley were engaged. Made from twigs of the maple he and Sammy planted in the Lord's Chapel rose garden, it was held together by rough twine and was perhaps his favorite of the many crosses in his life. Redemption, he thought, was everywhere if we're awake to see it.

He roamed to the closet and checked his cardigan pocket for the receipt for today's trip to the co-op and found the scrap of paper.

He had dropped by the Mitford library recently to return a book on Angus cattle, and knowing his predilection for quotes, Avette Harris had handed him this:

Men are worse than women in fretting over age.—Gabriel García Márquez

I've never known a woman who could weep about her age the way the men I know can.

Thurber had hatched the second acute observation.

Was Avette aware that he had a birthday coming up? Did she somehow know he was fretting about it? Did he look his age or even older? He hoped her overture was coincidental.

His seventies had certainly been a crossroads. He could

choose to be old, he had the credentials, or he could choose to be ageless, whatever that meant.

He was vain, really, something he didn't think most people suspected. How vain could a country parson be? And yet he was womanish in his alarm about wrinkles that appeared overnight. He would shave for decades over an untrammeled patch of skin and voilà!—suddenly there was a rut, a ditch, even several, never before seen. In his sixties, he had tried erasing such surprises with vitamin D oil, an act he practiced covertly, as if committing a sin of the flesh. But no, nothing would prevail against them.

'Look,' he said to his wife only a day or two ago. He had discovered a trench running south from the corner of his mouth to the lower realm of his chin. He hadn't often gone to her about the aging business. He wanted to seem above that.

'What?'

'This wrinkle,' he said. 'It wasn't there yesterday.'

'Oh, please, Timothy! I have dozens of those.'

He might have insisted otherwise, but he couldn't summon the wit for flattery.

'There are no easy fixes,' his primary care doc, Wilson, had said. 'Unless . . .'

'Unless . . . ?'

'Unless you want to have work done.'

He looked at Wilson in disbelief. That he would even mention such a thing to him was inexplicable.

'You'd be amazed how many men go for it. A lot, trust me.'

He leaned closer. 'Like who?' This should be rich. He had wondered a time or two about Mitford's mayor, Andrew Gregory.

He was unable, however, to wrest even one name from the man.

On occasion he had tried a new tie, more expensive and a tad more flamboyant than the ties of his middle years. That worked, of course, especially with a pocket handkerchief, a style not often adopted by clergy. But it worked for only a day or two, as he almost always wore his collar.

'I quit,' he had said to Cynthia.

'Quit what?'

'Trying.' That was all he was prepared to divulge, though he felt disappointed when she didn't press him for details.

When he had the need to talk to someone who would actually listen, his dog had been his go-to. Had Barnabas dozed off? No. Had he gazed around the room as others sometimes did? Never. His dog had kept his gaze fixed steadily on his master, as if he were entranced by every word, even those unspoken.

He walked down the back stairs in pajamas and robe and was surprised to see a light hovering above the porch glider. Lace's face was illumined by the glow of the iPad.

He had thought a bit of stargazing might be sedative, but no. At this hour, he should leave her to her privacy. He turned back to the stairs.

'Is that you, Father?'

'Sorry for the disturbance.'

'No disturbance at all. Come sit.'

'You're sure?'

'Please. I would love your company. I'm looking for my wedding dress. Cynthia offered to make one, but of course she can't sew.'

They had a laugh as he sat down.

'I've decided to look online for something totally gorgeous, that fits perfectly and makes my heart beat faster. For a hundred dollars.'

'A hundred dollars!' Having officiated at a few weddings in his time, he was savvy enough to be incredulous.

'It's a huge challenge,' she said. 'But I like challenges. The invitations went out today and we finally settled whether five o'clock is afternoon or evening and we're six weeks away and I have got to have a dress.'

She caught her breath. Addressing the invitations had been a wake-up call. 'I see it in my head. Very simple. Would like to have silk or a fabric like lawn or georgette.'

Lawn, georgette—these were words his mother, who sewed, had often used. 'They may not make those fabrics anymore.'

'Another reason it's a challenge!'

'You and Dooley are handling these life changes with great courage and humor. The farm, the cattle, the graduation, the wedding, the new clinic—all at once.' Unimaginable, but he wouldn't say that.

'We're completely nuts,' she said. 'We couldn't do it without everybody helping us. Not at all.'

She shut down the iPad and there was the light of the

waning gibbous moon. They didn't talk for a while; crickets chattered, Bowser yipped in his sleep.

'We wanted to tell you for a long time but knew it would be hurtful,' she said. 'Having children was the first really big thing we ever agreed on. A year later, we agreed on four. It was wonderful to dream like that, it helped us get through vet school. I felt so ashamed when I found out, ashamed that I couldn't make that happen for him, for us. In many ways it was like a death, four deaths at once. So much loss—his siblings lost all those years, and now this. I thought he might want someone else, someone who could give him an unbroken family. I wanted to die, Father, I really did. Cynthia said she had wanted an escape route, too, when she learned she would never have children.'

Nearly a half century in the priesthood and he couldn't find words. God will use this for good, he wanted to say. I promise.

There was a silence he felt responsible to break. 'Is the diagnosis a closed book?'

'That's what the doctors tell us. Hoppy, too.'

Closed books, either figuratively or literally, had no appeal. Indeed, he often kept a book lying open in his study so he could see the words or pictures as he walked by.

'I watched Mama die a little every day,' she said. 'I always thought death came at an appointed hour, but it came on daily house calls to the Creek. I remember the county woman was there Tuesdays and Thursdays. She would sit in the swing my father rigged on the porch and hum tunes she heard on the radio. She always said, *Your mama's dyin', we got to keep her comfortable.*

'But I thought if I tried hard enough, I could keep her alive. I was totally consumed by three things—keeping Mama alive, learning everything I could from books, and staying away from my father. I could not possibly have gone to school regularly and worn nice clothes and pretended.

'He never did the terrible things that my roommate Laurel's father did to her. You know I ran to Harley's trailer whenever I could; he was my funny, generous, secret angel. And I made that little nest under the house, where I read and prayed and did endless pencil drawings, and later I used to sleep there. It wasn't so bad, really, except for the spiders. Under the house with a flashlight, I went to Antarctica with Lord Shackleton, to Northanger Abbey with Miss Austen . . .'

'I remember you talking about Jacques Cousteau.'

'Yes, I loved following Monsieur Cousteau into the deep. I read everything the bookmobile lady chose for me, and then started choosing on my own. There were also books I didn't love at all but I read anyway, hoping to find something hidden and accidental that would change things.'

'Somewhere in there, you fell in love with Rilke, I believe.'

'Not in love, really, he was a project—during my sophomore year, I tried to translate his poetry into art. Perhaps all the dragons in our lives, he said, are princesses who are only waiting to see us act, just once, with beauty and courage.

Perhaps everything that frightens us, he said, is in its deepest essence something helpless that wants our love.

'I realized how much I wanted to act with beauty and courage, and how hard it is to do this. I almost managed to love the spiders.'

She gave him a smile, suddenly shy. She always opened up like this with Father Tim; she didn't know why and she couldn't seem to stop. He brought that out in people.

'I'm talking too much,' she said.

'Never!' he said, and she could tell he meant it.

'I'm so glad you caught me stealing Miss Sadie's ferns, it was truly meant to be. I'm grateful that you and Cynthia invited me to live with you, though I couldn't leave Mama. You let me know there was a way out if I really needed it. And then Mama died and you and Cynthia and Olivia promised it was not my fault, it was just the perfect and incomprehensible timing of God.

'Mama dying was hard, but it saved my life. I was like a chick hatching from a dark shell into a new world.

'And now all this—the wedding, the farm, everyone being together like family. A lot of times it seems like a dream. But I know what it is. It's grace. Totally.'

'You're precious to all of us,' he said. 'You've helped our son become a thoughtful, deeper man. You've touched us in ways that make us better.'

He could say it now, this truth that must be told. 'God will use this loss for good. I promise.'

There seemed nothing more to be spoken. They were quiet amid the symphony of crickets and night birds.

Little by little, he was gaining helpful information.

'So, what is Dooley wearing?' he said over breakfast.

'A white linen shirt, khaki linen slacks, and loafers,' said Lace.

'With socks?'

'No socks.'

'Ha!' From now on, he would get the skinny on such matters from the horse's mouth.

As for music, Dooley's old friend Tommy from Mitford School was a great guitar and mandolin player who was in a group called the Ham Biscuits. They were pretty famous in these parts, and this would be a freebie.

As for the Potluck Paranoia so recently broken out in their household, it was unanimously decided last evening after supper that they'd leave this conundrum to God and be completely happy with whatever turned up.

He'd been glad to say, in Baptist fashion, 'Amen and amen.'

Wed. Can there be such a thing as too much love? I am serious about this. I am filled with all the love for D that I

was never able to give to my mother or my father or my brother or anybody. And so I love D with all this held-back love. Is it overpowering to him? Is it too much? I am certain that God does not ask himself these stupid questions, He just loves us.

He called late last night and I was so worn out and crazy and he was too and we just went to sleep with each other on the phone. Okay, so that was a waste of money. I do not care. Just to be doing the same thing at the same time with him was a beautiful communication. Amazing that we woke up at the same instant around two in the morning. He said, "Whoa. Hey, girl. I love you."

Thurs. Irene McGraw called today. She said her twin sister Kim Dorsay, the film actress, loves the painting Irene bought~ she sent Kim a pic from her iPhone~ and that Kim is doing a beach cottage in Malibu and would like to see my work. If I would ever say it, which I will not, I would say OMG!! I will take pics and email to Irene. Will send my portfolio too. Even if it is old I think it's some of my best work.

Fri. D says he is partying down and all the girls are crazy about him. So strange that a year ago it would drive me nuts if I knew he was out partying, but now I know he loves me so much that nothing could ever happen. It's almost scary to know he loves me like this.

Made barbecued ribs tonight. I cannot believe it. I have

never done it before. People practically licked their plates. I should truly be vegetarian but maybe later.

Sat. To church in the morning to worship at Lord's Chapel and see Father Brad. We all try to clean our country selves up as best we can. When we don't go to LC, Fr Tim celebrates Holy Communion here and sometimes Evensong. I love Evensong, especially when the crickets are out. I am glad we don't do Lauds and Prime!

I have never seen so many ugly dresses. I cannot find this dress, which was woven out of daydreams and naiveté. I am not giving up. When I am too tired to do anything else I am searching for my dress. Hello, dress of my dreams! Please be out there!

Four

S he rolled onto her back and laughed. How perfect. How perfect! There was no other word. 'Thank you!' she said. 'Thank you, thank you, *thank you.*'

She had waked up knowing exactly what it would be, as if the idea had created itself in her dreams. She had hoped to give him a yellow Lab puppy or maybe a Golden, but hadn't been focused enough to make this happen. Which was good, because there was too much going on right now for a puppy.

This new idea meant that nobody would be allowed in her room until after the wedding, especially Dooley. She had the old key in a jar on the bookshelf. She would lock the door every day and wear the key around her neck on a chain with the cross he gave her the year of the great Christmas snow.

She sat up and blinked, dazzled. For some reason, this idea was her first truly deep connection to the huge change in their lives. The thought of making his gift also made it all real; she couldn't wait to begin.

But she couldn't begin today. Lily was dropping by at seven-thirty this morning on her way to Wesley and had something 'important' to discuss.

'Is it about the wedding?' she had asked when Lily called last night.

'Honey, everything's about th' weddin'.'

Later Olivia would drive out with lunch, and she and Olivia and Cynthia and Marge would make bow ties for the dogs. Then they'd drive up to see Clarence and Agnes at Holy Trinity and talk about the lovely gift Clarence would carve for every guest.

Tomorrow was her day for food shopping in Wesley. What she needed to pick up was only a block away from the grocery store. When she got home, she would carry in the shopping, then carry everything else up the back stair to her studio.

She ran into the small room with the door on which she had hand-lettered *Poudre*, and brushed her hair and applied blusher and lip balm, then wriggled into her oldest jeans and threw on a shirt and sweater and slipped into her sneakers.

She took the Dooley book from the shelf, opened it hurriedly, and wrote:

> *Woke up and there it was~ everything I needed to know about D's wedding present!*

She added what Father Tim liked to say.

> *Deo gratias!*

She was so excited she could throw up.

She ran downstairs, smelling the coffee. Yes, yes, yes, yes, yes, yes, yes . . .

'Do you know how much work a potluck for fifty people will be?'

Lily looked totally serious.

'I've been to lots of potlucks,' said Lace.

'But have you ever done one?'

'Never.'

'Me, either,' said Cynthia, who could feel a tempest brewing in the household teapot.

'I've been workin' here regular ever since you an' Father Tim hired me nearly seven years ago, an' now y'all an' th' Owenses are like family. So let me just tell you. You think a potluck weddin' will be the easiest thing you ever did in your life, right?'

'Well, yes,' said Lace.

'But you will be deeply disappointed, trust me. Lord knows, I have tried to keep my trap shut about it, but I cannot hold it in another minute.'

'Go for it,' said Cynthia.

'Work, work, and more work is the underbelly of th' whole potluck scheme. If you don't have organized help, you will be dead th' next day or wishin' you were. How many platters and bowls and pots and plastic containers will roll in

here? How many will not have a lid or a top or any ID whatsoever on the bottom?'

There was no known answer to this.

'How many will ask for leftovers to take home? Wait till
you see how many!

'How many rolls of foil and Saran Wrap will you go
through while people stand there tappin' their foot? How
many will be ticked off that nobody ate what they brought,
and how many will be pouty that people didn't leave anything for them to take home?'

'Clearly we don't know,' said Cynthia.

'Plus if there's nothin' left of what they brought, they will
want their platter, pot, pan, bowl, or plate back *washed*, and
that's not to mention th' rented dinner dishes.

'Rented dishes is not th' same as throwin' paper plates in
a smelly garbage can an' settin' it on th' truck to be hauled
off to parts unknown. You will be scrapin' an' washin'
dishes till the cows come home from Mink's place—which,
trust me, will be a long time, since Mink also has a bull
that's pretty cute.

'Plus, who'll be carryin' th' dirty dishes all th' way from
th' barn to th' kitchen sink? Per head, that's two glasses, a
cup, a saucer, a dinner plate, an' a salad plate. Times fifty.

'*Plus* there's all th' glasses people will be drinkin' out of
before an' after dinner. They'll be up in your barn loft an'
down in th' stalls an' lyin' out in your grass . . .'

'Good grief,' said Cynthia. 'The people?'

'Th' glasses. And who'll put th' rentals back in their crates for th' rental people on Monday? Th' plates, th' silverware, th' dirty napkins, th' tablecloths—I could go on.

'So, please, do *not* try to do this by yourself. I can get all my sisters out here and none of th' family will have to lift a finger. As hard as y'all have worked, nobody needs to lift a finger the day of this weddin', okay? Th' Flower Girls are ready to give you th' *break you deserve*.'

Lily sat back in the chair, satisfied. 'So tell me that that's not music to your ears!'

They hesitated a moment, somewhat stunned, then burst into spontaneous applause.

He heard most of Lily's sermon, with which he agreed wholeheartedly, but kept his head down. He poured a cup of coffee and checked today's corkboard pronouncements, these in Lace's quirky hand-lettering.

5 days till graduation!

6 days till Choo-Choo!

7 days till Home Eucharist!

8 days till grand opening!

FYI May 10 is Mother's Day

He was exhausted from reading the timeline. He declined to read the work list; he knew what had to be done.

Willie looked mournful. 'We'll be mowin' twice a week. I ain't never mowed twice a week.'

'Saturday an' Thursday is th' way I see that goin',' said Harley, who was known in Mitford for his lawn services.

As for his own observations, he quoted Uncle Billy from days of yore. 'There'll be no rest for th' wicked an' th' righteous don't need none.'

The lawn improvement was his wife's idea. 'Just this once,' she said, eager to finance the operation, gladly approved by Lace, as part of their wedding gift. He had pulled off the same deal on their lawn in Mitford; he was an old hand, he knew this stuff. Thus all supplies had been picked up at the co-op and starting today the three of them would initiate the program.

First they would use an organic spray on the weeds, which unfortunately amounted to the greater portion of the lawn, followed by spreading a load of composted material over the entire area.

This material would be raked in and seeded with a mixture of fescue, bluegrass, and annual rye. Then they would lime and fertilize and lightly straw the whole caboodle.

'Lord help,' said Harley, who offered his customers Mow and Blow only.

Willie was speechless.

As for moisture, they would have to keep their eye on it.

He pressed ahead with his tutorial. 'Comfortably damp but not too wet is what we'll be looking for.'

'This is a *farm*,' said Willie. 'Dogs pee an' kill th' grass. Chickens scratch around an' make dust bowls. Vehicles keep th' corncrib area half ruint. You can't have a town yard in th' country.'

As instigator of this project, he didn't include the astonishing news that there would be no more mowing grass down to the nub. Nossir, no more blade on grade. Three to four weeks from today, they would merely be taking the tips off, and by June fourteenth they would have a lawn ready for a magazine cover. A lot of work, to be sure, but all this run-up labor to the big day was suddenly the most fun he had enjoyed in a long time.

Okay, so everybody was a bit frayed, but everybody was also wired. There was joy in the air; you could sniff it as plain as new-cut hay.

She ran to the clinic with Truman following and talked briefly with Hal, Blake, and Amanda, their receptionist, scrub nurse, and all-around helper. Was there anything she could do? They were covered, but check back after lunch, if possible; two goats were coming in as well as the three Dalmatians from the Brewster farm.

Goats again! Though Dooley would be running a small-animal practice, he had recently relaxed that policy. 'We'll take anything that can get through the door,' he said. A horse couldn't really make it through the door, nor a cow, but sheep and goats, yes, and maybe even a llama if it ducked its head.

Four people in the waiting room—two with mournful hounds on leashes, one with a kitten in a carrier, and Lucy Bowman with her pig named Homer.

Homer was wise and thoughtful; she had known him for years. Homer sat on the bench next to Lucy, a proper good pig. She knelt by the bench and gave him a scratch behind the ears. She hated that Homer's eyes were cloudy now; she loved this pig.

'It's 'is kidneys.' Lucy blinked behind her bifocals. 'An' 'is teeth. They're fallin' out.'

Maybe one day pigs could be fitted with their own little choppers, which a kind owner might put in a glass of vinegar and water at night.

She gave Homer a hug and busied herself with greeting the other patients.

Whoa. There went Harley blasting out the back door, smelling like an Italian gigolo. Harley had bought this startling fragrance a few years back when he'd been enthralled with his landlady, Helene Pringle. Sitting moribund in a spray bottle for half a decade had done the aromatics no favor.

'And there he goes,' he said, looking out the kitchen window to the white Toyota with the ski rack.

At home in Mitford, they often sat in the study by their so-called picture window and watched the changing of the light. At Meadowgate, they were occasionally given to Reading the Sunset.

'Look!' said his wife. 'Coral growing out of a Pacific atoll.'

'Ah.'

'Don't you see it? Or maybe more like Chicago with fireworks over the canal.'

'An Arctic tundra, for my money,' he said. 'Except more colorful.'

They could also do this mindless entertainment with clouds. It didn't take much for them, not at all.

DR. AND MRS. WALTER ANDERSON HARPER

Invite you to celebrate the wedding

of their daughter

LACEY HARPER

to

DOOLEY RUSSELL KAVANAGH

Sunday, the fourteenth of June

Five o'clock in the afternoon

MEADOWGATE FARM

Farmer, North Carolina

POTLUCK, PLEASE AND THANK YOU

Casual ∽ Directions enclosed

Five

Two hams on the mornin' of a five o'clock weddin'? Are you sure you want to do that? This will be a busy kitchen.'

'So I'll bake the day before,' he said.

'It'll still be a busy kitchen,' said Lily. 'We'll have th' last of th' bread comin' out of the oven and three hundred cheese wafers plus Lord knows what else. Plus you'll be runnin' to Mitford to pick up th' cake, th' ice, an' th' guestbook that's shippin' to your house, remember?'

He felt a dash put out. 'So I'll work a five a.m. shift on the big day.' Didn't she know he was famous for baking hams for weddings, not to mention funerals? He needed somebody to cut him some slack.

Cakes. Ice. Guestbook. White vestments. The Local. He jotted down the aforesaid items in the planner he recently bought at the drugstore. Very handy.

With all that he'd been through as a working priest, he

had never had a planner. But then he had never been part of a family wedding—other than his own, of course, which he recalled as very, very simple except for the bride getting locked in her bathroom.

Lace had brought home last week's issue of the *Mitford Muse*, which he read with considerable savor.

He would check out the forty-percent-off sale at Village Shoes; he needed footgear for the wedding.

Six-year-old Grace Murphy of the curly hair was giving a tea party on Saturday to which all young guests and their moms, aunts, and/or grandmas were invited. The party would be held at Happy Endings Bookstore, reported Vanita Bentley, and afterward, 'the world-famous author, our own Cynthia Coopersmith (Kavanagh!!) will read one (or maybe two??) of her famous Violet books. 10% off every purchase if wearing a hat, yayyy!'

Esther Cunningham, former mayor and Absolute Mover and Shaker, was pictured holding yet another of her great-grans, the total of which numbered in the vicinity of Abraham's stars.

'Red Tape Holds Up New Bridge.' There you go. A close second to his all-time favorite *Muse* headline, 'Man Arrested for Wreckless Driving.'

As for hometown news in the raw, J. C. Hogan was now taking personal ads.

Not getting any younger—how about you?

Attractive Two-step seeks a Tango

And here was a new feature by the enterprising Ms. Bentley.

LOL

YOUR WEEKLY LAUGH

Selected by

Vanita Bentley

—When you go to court, you're putting yourself
in the hands of 12 people who weren't smart enough
to get out of jury duty!!

Right there was the only laugh some people would get this week.

No warning ever again about not planting till May fifteenth. Hessie Mayhew had retired to a bench in the sunshine of St. Augustine. 'Let people plant whenever they dern well please,' she said before pulling out last October in what appeared to be a Plymouth Fury hitched to a 5x10 U-Haul.

He folded Mitford's weekly gazette and left it on the kitchen table to be enjoyed by other inquiring minds.

He now understood why brides were often crazy, mothers hysterical, and fathers hiding in the tall grass. Each time one detail was settled, a dozen others reared their heads.

He called Dooley. 'Do we need to talk about parking?'

'Th' north strip. A couple of guys from th' co-op will handle parking. No problem.'

A good thing. He did not want to be directing traffic in the north strip with his vestments flapping in the breeze.

'Jack Daniel's or Wild Turkey to bury a month before the big day? Harley's running to town.'

Dooley laughed. 'Whoever digs it up won't be particular. An' hey, Dad, by th' way. We're going to set a place at the table for Miss Sadie.'

Lunch cleanup: LACE

According to the chalkboard, it was her turn, but Cynthia insisted otherwise. 'You look pale,' said Cynthia. 'Are you all right?'

'I'm okay.'

'Run up to Heaven and let me do this.'

As much as she needed to go to Heaven and work on his present, she needed something else far more—room to think about the phone call she just received.

She pulled on her jacket and walked across the yard to the bench Willie built, stopping along the way to deadhead the iris. That she had iris to deadhead was a marvel. She liked the crisp, clean snap as the spent blooms spilled their wine on her fingers. Olivia had taught her a lot about gardening, though she hadn't realized it then.

No matter what, she couldn't pass by the chickens, who, fond of the pleasures of free range, were latched in their run till after the wedding. There would be no feasting on expensive grass seed or scratching about in the straw. They came running to the wire fence, curious to find whether her hand would vanish into a pocket and come out with cracked corn. Yes! Into the air rose a shower of yellow morsels, catching the light and falling . . .

She sat on the bench and gave herself to a chill May breeze from the mountains that had consoled her since childhood. Even at school in Virginia she had never been out of sight of the Blue Ridge. It was real estate privately owned in her soul.

Over by the tree line the girls browsed fescue and clover. She counted them whenever she looked their way, making sure no one was missing.

'Take time to look at the view,' Beth advised when they talked yesterday. Her best friend and roommate from school would be coming from Boston with her mother, Mary Ellen, instead of with her husband, Freddie, who had walked out last Christmas, not even taking his clothes. Beth had been raised on a farm in upstate New York and knew a lot about natural beauty but hardly anything about men. As for Dooley's friends who were coming, there was only Tommy, who played mandolin and guitar and banjo and used to live up the street from the rectory. Dooley really wanted to keep the wedding small and have his school friends visit when things were more settled. She knew them all, she would like that; some had kids now.

She fidgeted with her phone, took a photo of the cows in the green distance, and sent it to Dooley. She had come out here to try to arrange things in her head before she called him, but she couldn't think and she couldn't wait. She needed to hear his voice now.

He was tossing stuff into a giveaway pile; she heard a Dave Rawlings CD playing in the background.

'It looks possible!' she said, startled by her tears. Funny how people are surprised when prayers are answered. 'They called early this morning. A few days before the wedding, they think. But they're not sure.'

'This is good.' He was hoarse with his own feelings or maybe exhaustion or actually both. 'Don't worry.'

She felt the commingled rush of joy and fear. She could hardly believe it was happening at last, and yet the timing . . .

This was a hugely delicate situation. How would all the wedding commotion at Meadowgate affect Jack Tyler? It had been close to impossible over the last two years to keep such an enormous secret from their parents, while the Owens and Willie and Lily, even Beth, knew everything. In its own way this had been as intense as their commitment to vet school.

'We have to stay calm.' She gulped a breath. 'We cannot

get crazy.' She was already a little crazy, but was doing all she could to hide it.

'Let's put craziness behind us,' he said. 'And about the weather—it should be against house rule to stress about it. If it rains, we get wet. So what, we'll remember it.'

Truman leaped onto the bench and made himself at home in her lap.

'Great. Okay. Yes.' She breathed out, let it go; she had to let it all go. 'It's beautiful here. We're getting rain tonight.'

'Love you,' he said.

'Love you back.'

'Miss you.'

'Miss you more.'

She would say how much more, but it was impossible to put into words.

'How are the girls?'

'I just sent you a picture. If they only knew who's headed this way!'

They laughed together. She was getting her breath back. 'Wait till you see what Clarence is doing for the guest gifts. Amazing. It's a really big order; two other carvers are working with him, they'll deliver the Friday before.'

She was dying to tell him about his wedding gift; he was her best friend and it was strange not to talk about it. She stroked Truman, gave him a neck rub.

'We decided about the dancing,' she said. 'If we get married on the porch, Harley and Willie will take the chairs away while supper happens in the barn. So, dancing on the porch!' With ribbons and roses twined on the railings and lights sparkling in the trees and lanterns flickering around the yard like fireflies.

She wanted to feel like a firefly herself on the night of their wedding. If she could just find a dress.

He liked sitting with Cynthia in the glider, which did indeed glide. Smooth as silk for an old hand-me-down, and a perfect way to savor the evening downpour on the tin porch roof. He could hardly wait until tomorrow to see how the grass was coming along.

Nearly two years had passed since his wife had labored over the writing and illustrating of a Violet book—or any book. She seemed content these days to observe all manner of activity without being stirred to put it between covers. Chickens ruffling their feathers and dusting themselves, old dogs sleeping, quail mothers followed by their obedient broods—in times past, any sort of farm life would have had her up and running to the drawing board. Her contentment was a turn of events completely foreign to him and he loved it. Now he was the only child, as it were, enjoying the best of her daily affections. She had absolutely adored creating all those books, she said, yet nothing charmed or drove or inspired her to do it again.

She had been known to channel leftover energy into all manner of unexpected things, once laying waste with a hammer to the plaster of their kitchen walls, then finishing them after the manner of 'ancient Italian villas.'

'So what do you want to do?' he said. Maybe more readings at bookstores—she liked that sort of thing.

'I want to . . .' She was pensive, choosing her words. '. . . *live*. Just that. Helping the kids get ready for the wedding, sitting here on the glider, making bow ties for the dogs—I'm finding all that enough.

'Then there's sleeping with my husband and listening to rain on a tin roof. Greatly enough!'

'Anything else mulling around in there? Some deep, ungratified desire?'

'The RV trip, remember? I'd love to do that. See the Oregon Trail, the national parks, I don't know. Wear a ball cap and jeans, sit in the passenger seat and knit . . .'

'You don't know how to knit.'

She laughed; he took her hand and kissed it.

Their moderately old marriage burned with a steady flame, and that too was greatly enough.

Having sent a link to Olivia and Beth, she took her iPad around to everyone she could locate.

'What do you think?' she said, showing them a full-screen image. As for her own thinking, this dress was only sort-of-maybe-kind-of, but she could be wrong. She was getting the desperate feeling that a lot of her bride friends had experienced in their search for the perfect dress. Of course they had started earlier and hadn't refused the help of their mothers, who were deeply invested in getting it right.

Father Tim moved his glasses down his nose and peered at the subject of interest. She figured he had seen a few brides in his time, he had good taste, he would know.

'More than a hundred, I wager.'

'Less!'

Cynthia was grating cheddar for her famous pimiento cheese.

'What do you think?'

'I'll be darned. Smocking! We never see smocking anymore.'

'Vintage,' she said, defending it somehow.

Lily weighed in. 'Looks big through th' waist. If it don't fit, my sister Violet can fix it. And if she can't, Arbutus can. Arbutus is married to Junior Bentley.'

'I know.'

'And lives in a brick house,' bragged Lily for the hundredth time, 'with two screen porches.'

Beth's review was totally brief.

No!

Olivia's e-mail was diplomatic. *You will look beautiful no matter what you wear.*

Nobody liked this dress, herself included.

Bummer.

Willie had bushhogged the north strip today and would mow it with a lawn tractor on the fourteenth. As for himself, he and Harley had finished getting the floor timbers in, shop-vacc'd the loft and old grain room, and weed-whacked around the barn—a job to be done again prior to the fourteenth. Then he and Lace had cleaned bird and guinea poop off a vast target site beneath the rafters.

'Look,' she said, beaming, 'I have calluses.'

'Do you like having calluses?'

'I do! I'm going to be a farmwife, you know.'

The Harley/Amber issue seemed to be fading from the collective household mind. Willie reported seeing the Toyota parked at the mailbox yesterday. Harley had gone out and stuck his head in at the passenger side but not for long, end of report.

'So what's going on with Harley and the Toyota?' he asked Lace.

'He's not talking.'

'Has he asked you about Las Vegas?'

'He said they'd talked about it, but she decided she couldn't leave her cats.'

'Is his money in a shoe box or in the bank?' He was a meddlesome son of a gun, a prime requirement for clergy.

'In the bank, in a CD, with something in savings.'

'What's this about her being a hoofer?'

Lace laughed. 'I meant to tell you. He said she danced in a show on Broadway years ago.'

Broadway? If that didn't take the cake . . .

The burial of the bottle had roused a good bit of merriment in what had been a hectic day. He and Cynthia were in bed by eight. Indeed, the entire ménage was quiet, though he heard the house phone ring a few minutes ago.

Graduation tomorrow. He would make breakfast and they'd head out with Lace around noon. Yesterday Lily had lined up the men, including Hal and Blake, and given them all a haircut on the porch. Though he felt positively skinned, he was ready to see Dr. Kavanagh *walk*.

They turned out the lights, silent for a time.

'Are you dead yet?' asked his wife.

'Not yet,' he said.

She placed the phone on the charger. Her whole body was thrumming with a kind of low-grade tremor.

She had just sold five paintings to a three-time Academy Award nominee on the other side of the continent.

Six

She would miss her lookout tower.

And sometimes she missed the children she had worked with at the nonprofit. She looked around the attic studio, at the walls hung with more of their art than her own. Luke's wild, painted horses. Emmy's huge raccoon faces. Eugene's skyscrapers and whirling Van Gogh planets. Latisha's row of strangely beautiful dolls . . .

When she and Dooley moved into the second-floor bedroom after the wedding, the view would be lovely but different. From this big attic window, she could look into the front yard and over to the clinic, and there was the green post in its bed of zinnias, waiting for the sign to be hung.

She went quickly to the other window, which was open to the breeze. The trailer was backing up to the cattle gate right now.

There was Jake from their hole-in-the-wall diner in Farmer. And their postmistress, Judy, who had been kind to them over their years of visiting Meadowgate. And there was Willie and Harley and Hal and Blake and Father Tim and Cynthia and all the farm dogs and a squad of neighbors lined up along the fence. How amazing! Their new bull was a complete celebrity.

She'd been working on Dooley's wedding present and forgotten the time, and if she didn't hurry, she would miss the whole show.

She tossed her hair into a ponytail and opened her jewelry box and took out the strand of turquoise beads. She loved these beads. He had given them to her when they finally knew the friendship ring was an engagement ring. She wore them only on special occasions, the most recent being his graduation yesterday.

And there was her cell phone ringing. That would be Dooley saying *Where are you?*

She slipped the strand of beads around her neck, fastened the clasp, and raced downstairs.

Yes!

She heard hooves thundering against the metal of the trailer bed, then clattering down the ramp.

Surely he would bolt into the pasture from the restraint of the trailer, but he stopped just beyond the ramp, silent as stone, looking ahead.

She drew in her breath, astonished by the authority of his massive shoulders and his immense poise.

He flicked an ear.

'Holy cow,' whispered Honey Hershell. 'That's some big guy you got there.'

Standing with his rump to the crowd in what Dooley called the 'chill pen,' Choo-Choo turned his head and gazed to the right, then turned his head and gazed to the left.

'Go, Choo-Choo!' yelled eleven-year-old Danny Hershell. But Choo-Choo stood motionless.

'Man!' said Jake. 'Last time I saw that bull, he was chasin' Emmet Holder through 'is turnip field. Emmet vaulted th' fence and hit th' road runnin'. I braked my truck an' he jumped in, said, *Floor it, Jake, that bull's out to get me*.'

'Judy's wearin' red,' said Honey. 'She better step back from th' fence, don't you think?'

'It's okay,' said Lace. 'I looked it up. Bulls can't distinguish red or green. It's the matador's cape that drives them crazy.'

'Here's y'r sign,' said Harley. 'It come on th' trailer with Choo-Choo.'

BULL IN FIELD

KEEP OUT

'I'll jis' lean it right here an' me an' Willie'll git it on th' cattle gate when th' truck clears out.'

'Don't you worry,' Jake told her, 'it's th' gentle bull, not the bad guy, who most often kills or maims 'is keeper.'

Honey was incredulous. '*Kills? Maims?* Are you kidding?'

'Wikipedia,' said Jake.

Choo-Choo faced the crowd now, with an unwavering stare.

'Whoa!' yelled Danny. 'He's lookin' at us, he's gon' charge.'

Choo-Choo tossed his head, ambled away, and began to crop grass.

The co-op manager removed his cap and scratched his bald pate. 'This ain't th' same bull as Choo-Choo.'

'Yeah,' said Danny. 'I could ride this ol' bull.'

Several onlookers had moved from the fence, were saying their goodbyes, congratulating Dooley and paying respects to his future bride. They had come to see a show and didn't get one, and she was relieved. She had dreaded whatever tricks this creature might be up to.

The crowd stirred, had a laugh here and there, slapped one another on the back. There was Harley, toothless as a crone and shaking hands as if running for county office, and Willie still peering into the chill pen hoping for a matinee performance.

She felt his arm around her shoulders and looked up.

'Hey,' she said.

Dooley drew her to his side. 'There you go. Your pet bull.'

She could feel his heart pounding. 'When does he get to meet the girls?'

'First he gets five or six days in th' pen. He needs to get used to being here. He'll probably walk th' perimeter of th' fence a few times, checking for a way out. But there's no way out, I guarantee it. Clean water, healthy grass, a little clover. He'll have a good life at Meadowgate.'

She looked at the set of Dooley's jaw, his determined gaze. Laughing, exhausted, working over a sick or wounded animal, whatever—he was beautiful in a way that had nothing to do with looks, in a way she believed only she had eyes to see.

'On th' fourteenth,' said Willie, 'you gon' be lookin' at a full moon.'

'Yayy!' Clapping around the supper table.

'If it don't rain and hide it.'

'Bo-o-o! Hiss-s-s!'

Willie grinned. He liked to stir up this crowd.

But she couldn't find it.

It was either backless or had an uninspired neckline or the fabric was synthetic or it cost too much or it was just *wrong*.

Why was she punishing herself with the idea of a hundred-dollar dress? She would not touch the amazing amount of money that would be wired into her account on receipt of the paintings, but she could put a For Sale sign on her ancient BMW and park it in the lot next to the post office or dip into her savings just this once. She would never make this special journey again; this was her *wedding*. Finding her dress should be a fun, even extravagant experience. But she didn't want extravagant—she was extravagant on canvas, and that was enough.

Having grown up with nothing, she might have spent all the money Hoppy and Olivia had provided along the way. But she had saved like a miser; the old I-will-never-be-poor-again scenario was real to her. Dooley was generous with his money but careful, and he had a stopping point—he knew how to think about the future. She was thinking about the future too, though most times it appeared in her mind as a complete blank.

'That's the way the future should appear,' Olivia once said. 'We're asked not to fret about the future and to take no thought for tomorrow. We must try to live in the present or we shall miss it entirely.'

Living in the present was exactly what she'd been trying to do. She wanted to totally show up for this incredible time in all their lives. She had two friends who remembered practically nothing about their weddings. 'I remember starting the walk down the aisle with my dad and I just blanked out,' Lisa said. 'When I sort of woke up, Tony and I were dancing. I was, like, are we married, what happened?'

The days were flying by. Everybody was constantly in a buzz, and as much as she loved living together as a family, she would be glad for a quiet house after the wedding, for just being with Dooley. They'd hardly had a minute together except for yesterday in the car driving back from graduation, where she and Cynthia and Olivia had cried as if it were a funeral, which it was in a way, with all the goodbyes and that big chunk of their lives being over.

Now they were looking at the grand opening on Monday and Dooley coming up on his first scrotal hernia procedure, this for a ram lamb, on Tuesday. So it was a lot, but he loved his new practice, which just happened to be unusually busy right now. Already he could not get enough of the life they had been waiting to live.

'Do *not* remove your dentures outside your room *at any time.*' She felt like a schoolmarm with a ruler.

Harley had lost his teeth again, and she was sick and tired of the let's-all-hunt-for-Harley's-teeth routine. Had he left them on top of the woodpile, as he had before? In the barn? In the glove compartment of his truck? Under the bed? On the roof? Maddening. Harley Welch was sixty-seven years old. When would he grow *up?*

'Grow *up!*' she said. '*Find* your teeth.'

Harley saluted.

'*Wear* your teeth.'

Boy howdy, ol' Dooley would be havin' hisself a handful.

He could still feel the grinding crush of the national board exam in December, then the long wait to learn whether he passed, whether he knew how to deliver the goods. So, okay, he knew and he had passed, but what it had taken to get here was still compacted in his bones. He stretched, drew in a long breath, and let it go.

He wouldn't want to be seen lying in a field, even though it was finally actually his field. He hadn't sprawled in the grass since grade school; bugs were not his favorite creatures on this planet. He hated to admit it, but he was zonked. He had been jumping through hoops for years, and now there were all the hoops to jump through this afternoon and to-morrow and the rest of his life. Okay, he really liked the hoops, all of them, but he needed a break, just a little time somewhere, somehow; he was running on fumes.

But even if they would spring for a honeymoon, they couldn't leave. No way. The practice was going full tilt and Choo-Choo had just come and he needed to get on speaking terms with this guy, which would take time.

Choo-Choo appeared pretty disgusted with Meadowgate—being restrained from what was clearly a larger world beyond the fence, being hauled to a strange place, and cropping grass that was different from the last grass he cropped. Who knew what went on in the head of a bull? Reading the mind of bovines wasn't something they taught at State. He would have to feel this guy out and let Choo-Choo do the same with him, and next week he'd be put in with the heifers, two of which should be ready to cycle.

He could see the calves coming onto the land, their herd

increasing. Lace would love that, he would love that. And Jack Tyler . . .

He closed his eyes and prayed his dad's favorite prayer, one he had learned to use pretty often in vet school. That prayer said it all when he had nothing left to say.

The smell of clover, the powdery fragrance of spring air, the gentle gurgle of Shallow Creek . . .

He couldn't know that his heifers stood bewildered in a group just yards away, eyeing his prone, sleeping body in the meadow grass.

He'd been mighty pleased on Wednesday when Mink Hershell stopped by to comment.

'Hey, Father, you can quit your day job and just do grass!'

Already poking through the straw. Already making a good show.

'The worst is behind us,' he said to Harley and Willie of the entire pre-wedding improvement plan.

'Right,' said Harley. 'It's jis' maintenance from here out.'

'Piece of cake,' he said.

Willie shook his head in the negative. 'We gon' need a hay baler.' They had refused to listen to his rain predictions, had planted bushels of grass seed without asking his say-so, and had completely taken over the old grain room where he had set up his private office with a busted recliner, a 1978 feed-store wall calendar, and a card table. Not that he needed an office, but still . . .

She was going to Wesley in the farm truck to pick up shipping material for the five paintings. It would take a ton of stuff to make them secure for the trip to California. Thank goodness Cynthia had done this a hundred times and would help her.

She drove past the clinic and looked at the sign they hung at high noon on Monday with everyone clapping and drinking lemonade and Harley ringing an old cowbell. Some came with their dogs on leashes, two showed up with cats in carriers, and there was Homer wearing a bandana and sitting up in a Red Flyer wagon. People had really turned out to congratulate Dr. Dooley, whom they'd known since he was a kid with freckles and a red cowlick shooting up like a geyser.

Painted beneath the dark green silhouettes of a dog, a cat, a sheep, and a goat:

KAVANAGH ANIMAL WELLNESS CLINIC

Dooley Kavanagh, DVM

At a time when so much seemed like a dream, the joy of the grand opening had been wonderfully real. Now it was time for her to be real. What if she couldn't find a dress? And what if she just wore something old, with new shoes? The whole thing was driving her insane, and everybody else, too.

How stupid to have pursued the ridiculous notion of a hundred-dollar dress while the days blew by like a rocket train. Now she really didn't have time to search around on the Internet. Nor could she make a desperate call to Beth to borrow her elaborate dress, because Beth, who was her size, had sold it on eBay the day after her derp husband walked out. She remembered Laura's extreme creation, bought by her dreadful father for nine thousand dollars without the veil—anything, of course, to make up for what he could never, ever make up.

So when she spent those few months modeling for Neiman's in Atlanta, she had bought a really beautiful white shirt. It was the white shirt she thought every girl would dream of having. She had worn it to work a lot because it looked so smart. When it picked up the tiniest stain or smudge, she removed it with lemon juice and sunshine until it was snow-white again. Then she let it drip-dry in her bathroom the size of a number ten envelope and ironed it as if it were holy vestments. She had always gotten the most compliments on it, and the older it became, the silkier it felt against her skin. She could wear that with her long white breezy skirt with a twine of Seven Sisters and stephanotis at her waist. She would put her hair up in a chignon and dress her hair with just seven of the Seven Sisters.

That would totally work.

And she would save a hundred dollars!

'Stop trying to protect, to rescue, to judge, to manage the lives around you . . . remember that the lives of others are not your business. They are their business. They are God's business— even your own life is not your business. It is also God's business!' Frederick Buechner

She transcribed the quote from Beth's e-mail into the Dooley book. She laughed. A very funny quote from some-body who was always managing the lives of others! 'I know,' Beth had said on the phone, 'but I'm trying to quit.'

She loved her best friend and figured the quote might come in handy at some point.

I have not been able to find any definition for cherish that feels special. It is really important to me to understand what it is because I love the word and think there's a rich meaning that has maybe been hidden or at least not much talked about.

Fr Tim says he feels cherish is linked to~ or perhaps best defined by the admonition in Romans 12:10: Outdo one another in showing honor.

Instead of parking at the corncrib after the post office, she drove to the cattle gate where Choo-Choo was standing. He looked mournful, somehow.

BULL IN FIELD

KEEP OUT

She jumped down from the truck and walked over to the gate.

'Hey,' she said.

She realized she was pacing the floor as if caged.

She was caged, in a way—by the enormity of everything, including the pressure of finishing Dooley's present on time. Somehow she needed to let it all go.

Let go and let God.

She had seen that sprayed on a wall of graffiti years ago and had written it inside the cover of her Dooley book. She had seen it hundreds of times when opening the book, so often that she forgot to consider the meaning anymore.

She found her pen and sat in the chair by the window and opened the book in her lap.

I give my wedding dress to you and also the weather on the fourteenth and the entire day and all the people who have worked so hard to make it happen and the people who will be coming. I give you Dooley's present and his vet practice and Choo-Choo and the girls and all the days of our wonderful life together in this beautiful place.

But most of all, Lord~ most of all~

I give you Jack Tyler.

Seven

Dooley stretched and sat up on the side of his narrow bed in the room adjoining what everybody called the glider porch.

If—just *if*—this was the day, would he be scared? He'd been best man in a couple of weddings where the groom had, on the big morning, immediately puked—not from last night's partying necessarily, but from fear. Sheer terror.

If this was the day, which it would be in just ten days, he would not throw up. He would not be numb with fear and he would not panic. What would he do?

He thought about it.

He would lie back down.

Oh, right. Given the fact that he was running a busy clinic, developing his herd, and doing his own spreadsheets for at least the first year, he would never again get a chance to lie back down.

She and Cynthia would be having yogurt and granola this morning. Father Tim would be driving to Mitford for his prayer breakfast and Dooley had called at six-thirty to say he was already at the clinic.

Today she would break in the shoes she bought to wear for the Big Knot. Strappy. Sort of a dressy wedge that wouldn't perforate the turf and cause her to tip over.

She brushed her teeth. Ten days and counting, and absolutely everyone would be coming. Not one single soul had sent or called in a regret except Louella, who they hadn't really expected since she didn't leave Hope House anymore. She had never heard of ninety-nine percent attendance, especially with people having to cook or bake and bring something. She loved their guests for pitching in like this.

Cynthia rang the attic at seven to say Father Tim had called from the rose garden at Lord's Chapel.

'He says there'll be buckets of roses on the Seven Sisters.' Buckets!

Little pails the size of a child's sand bucket. Not vases as they had planned. Placed in a long row down the table. Yes!

Ten buckets from the co-op, she wrote in her lined notebook. People used these sometimes for chicken feed. Wait. Fifteen buckets. And paint. And what about tablecloths? Why hadn't she thought of tablecloths before? Perhaps everyone was thinking rustic, barn, oil lanterns, bare wood, no tablecloths.

Well, yes, but they needed tablecloths for contrast; naked wooden tables would be lost from view in the barn aisle. Cream tablecloths, then. Five. Wait a minute . . .

She had a policy not to call him at the clinic, though he called her whenever he could. But this was different. She pressed auto dial.

How could this have happened? How could all those brilliant minds overlook something so obvious? What about Lily, who did this stuff for the mayor, for Pete's sake—what was she thinking?

She had just blamed it all on everybody else, which felt really good for about two minutes.

The real question was, what was she, Lace Harper, thinking? She felt she had sleepwalked through practically everything since pulling out of the driveway in Mitford. She had been a zombie, duh; everybody had been flying around trying to help the bride-to-be, who was, unknown even to herself, totally out of it.

'Hey,' said Dooley.

'Hey. Did you sleep?'

'Rock city.'

'When we said five tables pushed together in a long row, we forgot that we lose ten end seatings. Ten! Which means we have to add another table for ten, which makes the two ends of all the tables put together longer than the barn aisle, so somebody will be sticking out from under the shed on both sides.'

There was a stunned silence.

'Man,' said Dooley. He didn't want to ask her this, especially right now, but why couldn't a simple country wedding be simple?

'Lace is at the barn shooting pictures of Dooley's truck for some reason,' said Cynthia. 'But yes, this can be private. In case anyone comes into the kitchen, I'm taking the cordless to the library.'

'We got home late last evening from Hoppy's meeting in Denver,' said Olivia. 'How is she?'

'Calm as anything till the last couple of days. Bride Hysteria has set in. She just found buckets at an online hardware discounter and was going to paint them blue but remembered the lanterns are red and the roses are pink so that won't work and there are more tables than the barn shed will cover and she's working long hours on Dooley's wedding present, but what that is is an absolute secret. In a nutshell!'

She remembered her own Bride Hysteria, which started weeks before the wedding. And then an hour before the service, conducted by the bishop, the knob fell off her bathroom door and trapped her inside in a derelict bathrobe while two blocks away, the organ played for what Esther Bolick described as 'an eternity.'

'I have a wonderful idea,' said Olivia. 'But it's risky.'

Cynthia shut the library door behind her. 'I love risky.'

'If it doesn't work . . . I mean, we could present it in such a way that . . . But here's what I'm thinking. I was married in a beautiful gown . . .'

'You were the most gorgeous bride we'd ever seen, you took our breath away.' Actually, Olivia and Hoppy's wedding was the magna cum laude of all weddings, celebrating not only a new life together, but life itself, given Olivia's successful heart transplant.

'Thank you for that. There was a wonderful slip I wore underneath all that lace and tulle. A waterfall of pearl silk, lined in satin. Tiny straps. Asymmetrical hemline. I don't know why I didn't think of it before, but it's exactly what she's looking for. She's five-nine; I was five-eight and just her size, having lost so much weight after surgery. What do you think? Shall we pursue this?'

'Absolutely!'

'She's so earnest and works so hard and heaven knows, time is running out. If she really wants to wear a blouse and skirt, we can't stop her—she would be beautiful in a flour sack. All we can do is . . .'

'. . . suggest.'

Olivia laughed. 'Agreed!'

'I wore a turquoise suit for our wedding,' said Cynthia, 'so I haven't a scrap to contribute. How shall we proceed?'

'I remember your lovely suit. It had a silky sheen and wonderful buttons. Here's what else I'm thinking . . .'

She saw the UPS truck pull into the driveway and zoom around to the front porch.

She beat the delivery person to the door and, with four dogs barking, signed for the package and ran back up to the attic and waited until her heart stopped pounding from the round-trip on the stairs.

She didn't think she could bear to cram another secret into herself; she was stuffed with secrets. But she didn't want anyone else to see it until she gave it to Dooley ten days from now. She promised herself that she would not keep another secret for a very long time. 'Don't tell me!' she would say. 'I don't want to know!'

She tore off the wrapping and tossed it in the recycle basket and ran a palette knife under the tape that secured the lid to the shipping box and looked inside at the two signature pale-blue-almost-aqua boxes, Pantone 1837—and untied the white satin ribbons and lifted the tops and removed the velvet boxes.

She took a deep breath and sat on the side of her bed and opened the hinged top of the first box, and there was the beautiful gold band.

The painting she sold Irene McGraw had translated into something more real than money. She had never before made such a direct connection between her work and what it might afford her materially.

But she mustn't do this all at once. She was going too fast, she wanted to savor this, it was important.

She placed the box on her pillow and got up and poured a glass of water and took a pill for the pain, then sat again and removed the heavy gold band and held it in her palm for a moment before looking inside at the inscription. Perfect.

She opened the other box and removed a much smaller gold band and looked inside for its own inscription. The engraving was minuscule, but she could read it.

There had been no absolute certainty that this ring would ever be worn. But she had trusted.

She kissed the little ring and held it in her hand until it was warm from her touch.

Even with these last weeks of working outdoors, her husband looked oddly pale when he arrived home from Mitford at eleven o'clock. *Blanched* would be the word.

He set the bags from the Local on the kitchen table and headed upstairs to their room.

She gave him a few minutes and went up. He was sitting at the foot of the bed in a kind of daze. 'A call from Henry,' he said. 'I picked up our phone messages at the house. He's coming our way.'

'Henry!' she said, astonished.

'There's a convention in Charlotte for some of the people

he worked with on the trains. He was concerned that he hadn't heard from us. Living at Meadowgate has been like entering another world, I somehow lost connection.' He and Henry had written often; talked on the phone every week or so until he moved out to Meadowgate.

'This is great news!' she said. She had sat beside Henry's hospital bed in Memphis, when no one knew whether he'd live or die.

'He'll drive over to Birmingham to see an old friend, then board the Crescent up to Charlotte. He just got word from his doctor that he's good to go.' In the voice mail, Henry sounded plenty excited. This would be his first train trip since the transplant.

'He wants to see us. He wondered if we could come down to Charlotte, his treat at a nice hotel, he said. Or he can drive up to Mitford if that would be easier for us.'

He and Cynthia had talked through the possibility of a visit from Henry more than a few times. He had long ago known that he would introduce Henry not as his half brother, but as his brother. Period. After hosing his blood platelets into Henry's seven years ago, how could they be anything but brothers?

Could he feel at ease introducing his brother to Mitford? Just as important, how would Henry feel? And so what if neither of them felt completely comfortable with the social aspect of things? Was life ever perfect?

'I told him earlier that Dooley would be getting married,' he said. 'But I didn't mention a date, so he has no idea what's going on.'

'When would he be able to see us?'

'The thirteenth and fourteenth.'

She thought it was the perfect example of what southern-ers call a rock and a hard place. She sat beside him; they didn't talk for a time.

'When will you call him back?'

'Soon. Right away.'

'What are you thinking?' she said.

'He said it will be his last trip east.'

She was zooming along on his gift now, that's the way it worked—good days and bad days, just like people always said of a particular illness or travail.

And then there was the knock on the door and no one downstairs to answer it.

Down the steps, all twenty-two, and through the living room to the door and there was the FedEx person named Harry and four dogs barking.

PERISHABLE

She went to the kitchen and opened the package, a nearly impossible task just shy of breaking into a vault at Fort Knox, and there were two enormous beef tenderloins. Huge!

Love eternal,
Beth and Mary Ellen

Their first potluck had arrived.

'What are you worried about?'

'What do you mean?'

'I can tell,' said Dooley.

'Well . . .'

'Just . . . well?'

'I don't know,' he said.

'You sound like me.'

'Henry.' He removed his glasses, rubbed his eyes, breathed out. 'Henry is coming this way for a convention in Charlotte and wants to know if . . .'

Lord help him. He despised his fear, so deeply, viscerally rooted that he could not gouge it out.

'. . . if he can come for an overnight with Cynthia and me. The thirteenth and fourteenth. He didn't know the wedding date, didn't know we're living out here.' He wanted to fall down dead. Dead would be good.

But Dooley was ahead of him. 'We'll send Harley to bring him up.' Dooley was smiling, beaming, really—what a God-given sight. 'Henry can have Miss Sadie's place at the table. She would like that and we would, too.'

Dooley put his arm around the man who had believed in him, suffered his rebellious crap, given him love he didn't know existed.

'I can't say any more right now, Dad. But let me just tell you. We may all be in for a surprise at this wedding.'

His wife was winding down a tutorial before their nighttime prayers. Not to be missed in this life was a tutorial of any sort by Cynthia Coppersmith Kavanagh.

'And you simply say, This is Henry Winchester, my brother.'

'This is . . .' He was relieved and happy, though the tears were coming and he couldn't help it.

'. . . Henry Winchester . . . my brother.'

Eight

To say it was a perfect late-spring day could suggest that others gone before were not. Indeed, they had all been perfect for a long stretch, with just the right amount of rain.

The barn doors were closed to keep roosting fowl from targeting the aisle. The stalls were mucked, and the loft filled with fescue from the recent mowing.

Though often offended by the nonchalance of dogs, the zinnias had prospered; the impatiens gave the barn a certain panache; and new grass was flourishing.

On Sunday afternoon, Hal and Marge came over for a tour around the premises, for Dooley's deep-dish pizza, and Father Tim's Evensong. Afterward they all hung out on the porch just to watch the grass grow.

For additional amusement, there were the chickens, recently released from their run and pecking about with something like glee. And the swallows darting and diving through the lambent air, devouring insects and furbishing elaborate mud nests under the eaves.

It was a joy, they conceded, to look upon such vernal satisfactions.

She was not a child anymore. Those coming to the wedding would be their *guests*, they would be kind enough to bring *food*; she had to *prepare* for them and make them *comfortable*. Forget rain—what if it was a really hot day and they were all broiling in the sun while the vows were being exchanged and think of Father Tim in his heavy brocaded special vestments. Or if they used the porch for the ceremony, then all the chairs would have to be taken off the porch to make room for dancing and the musicians, which would be a scramble.

'We're having a tent,' she told Dooley. 'For the ceremony.'

He would be disappointed that she was not the hard-nosed pioneer woman in a sunbonnet ready to skin a squirrel and boil up a stew.

'Great!' he said. 'I'm for that.'

'We're having a tent!' she told the household, who had obviously wanted a tent all along. Of *course* everybody wants a tent! What is a summer wedding in the country without a *tent*?

She felt ten feet tall.

They would put the tent up on Saturday and take it away on Monday.

'You may want to order extra chairs,' said Cynthia. 'For the ceremony as well as for the barn supper. You never know. I mean, look at the marvelous surprise of Henry.'

'I'm not sure,' she said. Here they were splurging on a tent plus adding chairs.

'These things happen, they say—extra people show up.'

Okay, extra chairs. 'Six? Eight? How many? Does that mean an extra table? I mean, we're already sticking out on either end of the shed.'

'People will love sticking out on either end of your shed. You might order another table while you're at it, and oh, say, fourteen chairs. Seven is my favorite number, so I would say seven for the barn and the same for the ceremony, or you could pick your favorite number. Just in case.'

Duh, she didn't have a favorite number. So okay, fourteen.

She texted Beth.

> What about overalls with
> a white t-shirt? ☺

> > U do not want to
> > do that.

She upended the buckets on plywood laid across sawhorses. She would spray-paint them a soft cream color instead; blue would detract from the sweet stardom of the Sisters.

'Make sure no bulbs are burned out,' she said. 'Then we'll go ahead and string the lights in the trees and bushes.' While painting buckets she was also commandeering lighting for the trees and boxwood. She was a fan of multitasking.

'Who's gon' climb up in th' trees?' said Willie.

Willie had arthritis and Harley was nursing a recent knee injury.

'I will,' she said. 'Bring the extension ladder from the barn.'

'Dooley ain't gon' like you climbin' up in th' trees,' said Willie.

'We need t' git some young people in here,' said Harley.

'I am young people,' she said.

He wheeled into the driveway from the barber up the road. Meadowgate had never looked so good. It had the shimmering perfection that usually comes only after rain, everything sharp, clear, clean. The grass, the sign, fresh gravel on the drive, green rockers on the front porch, the flag flying from the porch column, new paint on the clinic door . . .

How long it might take for him to see it as theirs, he didn't know. In a way, it would always belong to Hal and Marge, who had been like parents to him. From no parents at all to three great sets of parents—it was beyond understanding.

His dad had put his heart and soul into the work done here in recent weeks. He had poured a lot of love into the place. Who knows how long love could last on a place? Maybe forever.

He wanted to be all that he needed to be—for Lace, for his patients, for his sibs, and certainly for—but he didn't want to think about that now, the situation was still uncertain. Maybe he and Lace had relied too heavily on everything working out.

All the commotion, the busy household, was a good thing, but he hadn't been prepared for it, he hadn't trained for it. It had come suddenly and sometimes he felt overwhelmed, caught inside a wave. He'd been amped for a long time; actually, everybody he knew was amped. He would like to spend the rest of his life de-amping.

He took the keys out of the ignition and came awake to the sudden longing for the peace of her, the long future of sleeping together, skin to skin. They would wade in the creek and fish in the pond, telling each other the truth about themselves, and maybe in a couple of years, there would be llamas with their confiding eyes. He would be with her forever; not even death would separate them. He thought that bit in the ceremony about 'until death do us part' should be rethought.

He pulled down the visor and looked in the mirror. The barber had sheared sheep for a living for twenty-four years;

now he had a bad back and was shearing people for ten bucks a head. Lace was not going to like this.

'I can't believe it,' said Lace.

'Skint,' said Harley.

'It'll grow out,' said Dooley.

As for their resident priest, Cynthia had eased up on him about haircuts. What was left of his hair in back was now growing over his collar and she liked it that way. Indeed, a curl or two had presented itself, possibly for the first time since childhood. The day before graduation when everybody got shorn on the porch, Cynthia had actually stood by Lily to make sure she didn't cut off his curls.

Wonders never ceasing.

A new list going up by the back door . . .

He would take Cleaning Out the Hen Boxes, as the contents would be good for the grass, and opt for Weed-eating the Pet Cemetery on the twelfth, all the while working with Lace on their homemade wedding program.

He had thought things would slow to a simmer, but no. Six days before *the* day, and the pot was still boiling.

'I'm running to town,' he told Cynthia on Monday.

'What for?'

He couldn't find a reason in his rattled brain. 'To, you know, just get *out* of here.'

'I'll ride with you,' she said.

They were all coming down with the highly contagious Bride Hysteria.

'I could have done it,' said Dooley, looking at hundreds of tiny lights strung in their two old maples and the boxwood. 'You should have let me do it.'

'I loved being up there.' She had peered into the window of the bedroom that would soon be theirs, and along the road to the Hershells' place, and seen Truman trotting across the yard as if on a very important mission.

'Great job,' he said. 'You're amazing.'

'Tonight after dinner, let's turn them on, okay? A rehearsal. Just us.'

'Deal,' he said.

Sweep, sweep, sweep.

Her hands had developed calluses over the last weeks. Since she was going to be a farmwife, which she wanted with all her heart to be, she would need calluses.

She loved to sweep, it was an act of redemption. All the dead bugs, grass clippings, dog hair, you name it, off the porch and into the forgiving grass

Dooley's palms, once 'book soft,' as he termed it, were also wearing in to rough work. When they held hands, she liked sharing this simple talisman.

Cynthia saw Lace moving toward the fence carrying a bucket, with Truman at her heels like a pup.

The window above their Mitford kitchen sink looked out to the hedge and the old rectory, which was never a bad view. Here she was served the shifting combination of sunlight and shadow over meadows animated by grazing cows. She had always liked the cow's noble acceptance of circumstance. A cow seemed to be saying, That's cool, I'm fine with that, whatever.

Lace appeared to be calling to someone. She moved to the right of the sink to see who it could be.

Choo-Choo.

At a gallop.

Good Lord, he looked ferocious chasing across the field at high speed. She knew a bull probably couldn't hurdle a fence, yet she was tempted to raise the window and yell, 'Stand back!'

And there he was; he'd covered the distance and reached the fence and Lace was stroking his enormous leathery nose.

Then Lace dipped her hand into the bucket and came forth with what must be the irresistible sweet feed, because a fourteen-hundred-pound Red Angus bull was eating out of her hand.

She was working with Father Tim on the wedding program, trying to make all the pieces come together and fit all the people into the right spots. As for Dooley's wedding gift, she was taking anything she could get: Fifteen minutes. Ten minutes. The occasional hour. She could not stop and fix every minor disappointment; she had to keep moving and stay open to what she was getting right now, at this moment.

Thank you, thank you, thank you.

He would love it, she was loving it. It would be the best wedding gift she could possibly give him. Not cuff links, not new work boots, not an oiled jacket from Orvis or even seat covers for his truck. Just this. Just this one true river flowing directly from her heart . . .

Harley was silent for a time. Whatever was stuck in his throat, it was like swallerin' down a golf ball.

'It's just two little lines on a piece of paper,' she said. 'Think of Sacagawea and what an amazing thing she did, and how you loved learning about Lewis and Clark and were so great with conquering arithmetic. Remember how happy it made you to jump over a wall of fear to learn new things.'

He wanted to bawl like a baby, but drew himself up like a man. He had never stood up in front of people and read anything out loud. If he didn't love this young'un . . .

'I'll do it,' he said.

She gave him a kiss on the forehead and a big smile and handed him a piece of paper with two lines typed on it.

He waited till she was out of the room before looking at it.

'Make their life together a sign . . .'

'Ten, nine, eight, seven . . .'

They counted down together as Harley waited to flip the switch at the light pole in the yard.

'. . . four, three, two . . . lights!'

'Wow,' said Dooley. The skin prickled on the back of his neck. 'Wow.'

'Good night, Harley,' she said.

'Same t' you 'uns.'

They sat on the top step of the front porch. A small breeze stirred, the lights glimmered. There was nothing to say for a while. She prayed, silent.

'Would you like to do our secret vows tonight? Like now?'

'Sure,' he said. 'Yes.'

They held hands, each silvered in light from the shining trees and half-moon.

'I will never leave you,' she said. She had been left by both parents, not physically—but mentally, emotionally, they had vanished before her eyes.

He was thoughtful about what she said, and grateful for the vow she had chosen. He took a deep breath and waited before giving his, though he'd thought it over carefully for days.

'I will never harm you.'

A chorus of crickets, the sound of a nightjar . . .

'I'll love you even when I don't like you.' She knew there would be such times; they had survived more than a few.

'And I'll love you even when I don't like you,' he said, for it was worth repeating.

'One more,' she said, looking at him in the light of the trees. 'I will love you always.'

If there was anything they hadn't confessed over the years, anything that troubled them about the other, they couldn't name it. He had a couple of buddies who hardly knew the women they were marrying. There was a time when he envied this—when he felt that he and Lace knew each other too well, where was the mystery? But he had passed through that phase and found that time made his love less tenuous, more certain. He had lived the last years of school in the cocoon of that kind of love. No longer did a brisk wind instill fear of a gale.

He figured that thirteen years of knowing each other could be divided into three categories. Three years of juvenile antagonism, followed by four years of fire and ice—a roller coaster that had flipped them both out. Then the last few years of falling into a new way of loving, a new way of doing things—yoked together, generally plowing the same furrow in the same field for the same reasons.

Just recently he had glanced at her and for a fleeting moment had the sense that he was seeing himself. Not the physical aspect of himself, but some inner aspect—who was who and which was which?

'I will love you always back,' he said.

He put his arm around her and they looked out to the haze of a half-moon, to dark summer trees where fireflies danced.

Nine

Violet, Delphinium, Arbutus, Iris, Rose, and Pansy insisted on standing while the household sat around the kitchen table during Lily's rundown of the final crunch.

'Okay, so guests will park on th' north strip and walk to th' house. They'll be jugglin' a fruit cobbler or a Crock-Pot plus a weddin' present an' a heavy pocketbook stuffed to th' gills. Now, that is a pretty good walk across th' north strip with all that plunder, an' some will be doin' it in high heels. Even if they know better, they will wear high heels, trust me on this.

'So finally they get to th' house an' what happens? They find out th' food table is in th' barn, which is a pretty good walk its ownself.

'So Willie, you an' Harley need to have th' farm truck shined up an' that blue quilt in th' bed—clean, if you don't mind. Okay, you need to park it at th' north strip and tell people to set their stuff in there—their weddin' presents, their covered dish, whatever. Then you and Harley drive down to th' house and offload th' presents on th' glider porch, where there'll be a table with a long skirt an' a vase of flowers—you have got to have flowers on th' gift table. Del, th' gift table is your job—do not even think about lettin' your back go out, plus you're on cleanup after supper.

'Then Willie an' Harley hot-rod th' food to th' barn an' offload it onto th' tables. Vi, it's your job to set it out—all breads together, all meat together, you know what I mean. Then after supper do a cleanup an' send everything but th' rentals to th' house. Arbutus and Pansy, you're on this detail with Vi. That is a big job, plus somebody has to mind th' flies. Harley, you mind th' flies.'

Lace realized that Olivia had been right about absolutely everything. But it was too late.

Willie squirmed on the bench. If Dooley an' Lace had young'uns, he would be dead and gone by th' time they were old enough to get married, which was just fine with him. As for rain, the weatherman was callin' for a thirty percent chance. 'What if it's rainin'?' That was the sixty-four-dollar question, and he was man enough to ask it.

Lily nailed him with a look but didn't miss a beat. 'So y'all know th' musicians are not bringin' food.'

Of course they knew that. Well, some did and some didn't.

'That is five big boys we got to feed, okay? So I am makin' a huge macaroni an' cheese. Huge, because these boys are huge. I have worked with th' Ham Biscuits at th' mayor's party more than a few an' they eat as good as they pick, you will not be disappointed.'

'Amen to that,' said Vi, who often sang and yodeled at parties, though she was not booked for entertainment at this event.

'Okay, that takes care of food an' presents. Now, here's where th' cheese gets bindin'.'

A few considered the cheese already as binding as they could tolerate.

'Th' men will immediately want to go to th' chill pen and look at your cattle. But *if*—just *if* it's rained, what'll happen?'

Nobody knew.

'We have to talk about this, okay?

'All around the gate there will be mud. And after the men have chewed and spit and maybe had a little shooter, they'll come up to th' house. Then they'll come *in* th' house without wipin' off their feet—think about it. They will come in because they don't need to go look at the chickens. So they will come huntin' their wife or girlfriend, who will be wanderin' up and down your halls goin', *Oh, look at that, if that's not darlin', I don't know what is, an' let's shoot us a game of pool while we're at it.*

'Pansy, you need to put mats down at every door, rain or shine. Those old mats rolled up under the stairs, they'll do fine, this is a farm. An' if nobody minds, we need to get some signs up. Signs are helpful on a big place like this. Harley, knock us together some wood signs an' keep it simple.

'Father, when you get a minute, you have a nice-lookin' hand, use a Magic Marker. We need one that says Chickens This Way—th' kids'll want to see th' chickens—one that says Dinner This Way, one sayin' Toilets—no, don't say toilets, just write Facilities with a arrow pointin' . . .'

Jiggling his leg was no longer an unconscious act—Dooley knew he was jiggling his leg and he was not going to stop jiggling his leg until he was good and ready. He was about to freak; anytime now he would bust out of here to check his cattle.

He and Lace and everybody else had done all in their power to keep it simple. They made their own invitations, saved a ton by not having a caterer or a tuxedo rental or an over-the-top bride's dress to drag around in the chicken manure. What happened to their laid-back country wedding where people could chill out, relax, no problem? Okay, so maybe there was no such thing as a laid-back wedding, no matter how hard you tried.

Dooley stood up, put on his jacket. 'Checkin' the stock,' he said, and blew out the back door. He had only one consolation—the absolute certainty that he would never get married again as long as he lived.

'Plus wait till you see how many want to drop off their dish in the kitchen so th' help can slice, bake, reheat . . .'

Lace placed her right thumb on her left wrist to check her pulse rate. They could have had the ceremony at Lord's Chapel, then driven to the club for dinner and dancing, and now she would not be exhausted and befuddled and ready to head upstairs and leap out the window. She had asked Lily to give them a rundown—she was great at giving rundowns—but this was out of control.

'An' that,' said Lily, 'is th' way this thing will roll.'

He was stunned. All the work they had done and all this still to do? The very act of opening his mouth to speak would be excessive in the extreme.

'And we thought we didn't have a wedding planner,' said his wife.

'Y'all remain for a meetin' right after this,' Lily told her sisters.

The rest of the assembly excused itself. Fled to other parts.

Four more days.

'On the mornin' of th' big day, protein is th' ace in th' deck.'

'Omelets with ham!' said Vi.

'No ham,' said Lily. 'Th' bride does not need puffy eyes on her weddin' day.'

'Omelets with kale would be my vote,' said Arbutus, who lived in a brick house with two screened porches and was married to Junior Bentley. She had been introduced to kale by a daughter who lived in Colorado and was different from the rest of the family, but hadn't she, Arbutus, gone online and looked up the benefits of kale and how you could cook with it and put it in salads and there you go, people in Colorado knew things not presently understood in these hills.

'Kale?' said Lily. It was a look of what Granny Flower called scorn.

Arbutus had long ago learned how to deal with Lily-big-britches: she let her much, much older sister have her way—that simple. Was Lily married to Junior Bentley, who was the greatest catch in the entire county? No. All Lily's catches had to be thrown back.

Plus, not only did Lily not have a house with screened porches, Lily Flower did not have a porch at all. If you were going to sit out at her house, you had to sit in th' yard. Plus when you went to visit, you stood on the top step in a drivin' rain poundin' on th' door and when she finally answered, you were soaked to the skin. No, she did not argue with her much, much older sister, she would not stoop to arguing. So forget kale.

'Omelets are labor-intensive,' said Lily. Why did these people not know these things? Why did she have to instruct them every step of the way, in every little bitty bloomin' thing?

'How many people?' asked Rose, who liked facts.

'Dooley, Lace, Father Tim and Cynthia, Harley, Willie, Sammy, Rebecca Jane, who's givin' a hand, Doc and Miz Owen, who're givin' two hands, plus Dooley's little brother an' sister, Jessie and Pooh, and Doc Harper and Miz Harper, who's takin' care of th' flowers, an' th' Father's brother and Lace's roommate from school an' her mother from Boston.'

Pansy counted on her fingers. 'That's sixteen.'

'Eighteen,' said Rose.

'Seventeen,' said Lily. 'So breakfast casserole with turkey sausage.' End of discussion.

'You'll need fruit with that,' said Vi. Didn't she have some say-so in this extravaganza, which had been draggin' on for a hundred years, including plantin' grass, buyin' cattle, paintin' baseboards, sweepin' barnyards, you name it? She and her sweetie, Lloyd Goodnight, had got hitched two years ago by a justice of the peace and gone to Arby's after. She hoped this would inspire others to adopt a simpler nuptial order.

He was washing dishes from their early supper, Lace was drying. He mentioned that Cynthia had seen Choo-Choo eating out of her hand. An amazement.

'I feel sorry for Choo-Choo,' said Lace. 'He has a terrible reputation and he's in a new home and I just thought he needed a friend.'

'Aha. So what's Harley up to these days? What's going on with the Amber business?'

'I think it's over, but I don't know. He won't talk about it.'

Someone yelling. He glanced out the open window above the sink. 'Holy smoke! It's Harley!'

They ran out, slamming the screen door, detoured the steps, and jumped off the side of the porch. With four barking dogs bringing up the rear, they reached the fence as Harley vaulted over it.

'God A'mighty!' yelled Harley, coming down hard in the grass.

'What were you doin' in that field?' asked Lace, back in the kitchen.

'Lookin' for m' teeth.'

'No way,' said Lace. 'What would your teeth be doin' in the field?'

'I dropped 'em, I don't know where at.'

She did not like this teeth business. She was not Harley Welch's mama. 'I'm up to *here!*' her own mama used to say when overprovoked.

'Okay,' she said, keeping her voice level. 'You know that nobody but Dooley and Willie are allowed in the field with Choo-Choo. Besides, teeth don't just fall out of their own accord.' Ridiculous! She was so over this.

'I run in there th' other day when th' cattle was layin' out under th' trees.'

'What for? Why did you run in there?'

'Me an' Willie was kickin' around a ball an' it went' over th' gate.'

'So when you went in to get the ball, your teeth just

dropped out of your *head?*' Why oh why was she doing this? She needed counseling.

'Dropped out of m' shirt pocket. Maybe. I don't know.' Harley rubbed his bad leg, glanced up to see if she was looking.

'Ugh,' she said, and left the kitchen.

Father Tim had to laugh. 'You're gettin' on her list, bud-dyroe.'

Three more days.

She ran to the clinic and entered by the rear door.

'Where's Doc?' she said to Blake, who was unpacking cat and dog food onto the shelves.

'Just washing up after—you don't want to know.'

'What?'

'A cat with diarrhea.'

She ran to the room with the big sink. 'Hey,' she said.

He grinned. 'Hey, yourself.'

He was drying his hands. It smelled terrible in here even though the exhaust fan was running on high.

She went to him and put her arms around his neck and kissed him, really kissed him. 'I love you, I love you,' she said. 'Gotta go.'

She raced into the reception room and grabbed the water-ing can from behind the counter and headed out to the zin-nias. She wanted the zinnias to look their best.

'Oh, Miz Kav'nagh!' An older man, wearing suspenders, looked up from a read in *People* magazine. 'Just wanted to say we sure appreciate your husband.'

She didn't say he isn't my husband yet; she said thank you.

'He's been so good with our Maizie. She's havin' her shots today.'

'Oh, yes, I'm so glad Maizie will be able to keep her food down now.'

'You know about Maizie?'

'Dr. Dooley talks about his patients at the supper table.'

'Oh!' The man colored with a certain joy. 'Kav'nagh. I don't believe we've heard that name in these parts. Is it . . . foreign?'

'It's Irish,' she said. 'A lot of Irish settled this area. What's your last name?'

The man stood and shook her hand. 'Randy O'Connell. Glad to meet you.'

'I believe you're Irish, too, Mr. O'Connell.'

'Call me Randy,' he said. 'I married Mink Hershell's second cousin on his mother's side, she was a Doughty.'

'I believe she may be Irish as well.'

'My goodness. Irish! Well, you come see us, you hear? We live up behind th' post office. But wait till August when th' tomatoes come in, I grow Big Boys. I know my wife would love to give you a glass of sweet tea and a tomato sandwich.'

'On white?' said Lace. 'With lots of mayonnaise?'

He gave her a big smile. 'And mashed down flat so th' tomato juice runs into the bread. It's th' only way.'

June 11~ Dooley has gone from college student to grown-up really fast. I think it's the cattle and the clinic. He is working long hours and is so sweet to everyone. His patients love him and I love seeing him work. He is very serious and intense.

I like what Hal said before D's graduation~ You go from all those years as a student to an actual vet instantly. Nothing gradual, just boom. Some get cocky and think they know it all. It can be a tough transition. But Dooley's been hanging out at Meadowgate for years watching us work and giving a hand. He'll have a pretty level head.

I think maybe I'm growing up, too. We will keep Lily on for two days a week. I will pay for L, who is priceless even if she does try to run the show. I need someone to help run the show.

His present is nearly done. It has to be done! There is no time to do more~ I am dying for him to see it. I can hardly bear to keep it a secret. Fr Tim will love it, too. Will take a pic with my iPad and send to Beth.

We need rain. Just not on the DAY, please! Dooley is worried about the pastures being dry.

Clarence is delivering guest gifts tomorrow~ I'm thrilled. Lots of raffia to tie on~ we will sit around the table after supper and do it together.

Harley has not found his teeth. We will launch one more major search and that does it! No more searches for teeth!

I went to the co-op yesterday because Willie forgot laying mash and there was Buster, who said the Golden puppy was spoken for and at his house waiting for the owner to pick up. If I had seen it first, we would have a new puppy, so I am relieved, I guess.

Buster said tell Doc Kavanagh hello.

I will soon be married to someone named Doc like out of a Western totin' a six-gun! This is really fun that I get to see D as Doc Kavanagh.

The lights in the trees are perfect. We are so happy. But worried too~ because no call yet. Thy will~

June 12~ Okay! Okay! I am finished! Time has run out and the light wasn't always perfect and it could have been so much better, but honestly I am always kicking myself for something. Judgment is God's job!!!

Done.

She sat on the side of her bed with the Dooley book in her lap, and exhaled. She felt as if she hadn't exhaled lately; all manner of delirium was stored in her chest and shoulders and neck.

She went to the window and closed it; the last couple of days had been cool enough for a sweater at night.

Then she remembered. Yes!

She dipped her brush in what was left of the cadmium red on her palette.

Lace, she inscribed on the finished product.

Then, Kav . . . an . . . agh . . .

She had heard people say that at a certain moment in their lives the earth moved.

As she finished writing what would be her new name, she felt that it sort of did.

He was taking off his clerical collar on the back porch, following a quick trip to Mitford for cleaning and mail.

'Can I bring a guest?' said Harley. He had talked to people who said sometimes you could bring a guest to a wedding.

'You'll have to ask Lace. It's pretty late in the game.' The other shoe was dropping on the Amber scenario. 'So, ah, who would you be bringing?'

It appeared that his old friend was—what? Blushing?

'Miss Pringle,' said Harley, looking him in the eye.

It was a sight to see. Lace Harper had pinned Harley to the kitchen wall—in a manner of speaking.

'*Where* in the field?'

'Summers around th' water trough.'

'Who are you sending in to find them?'

Harley looked over at him, desperate.

'Don't look at me,' he said, meaning it. He was busy replacing the stretcher of a kitchen chair.

'*Who?*' said Lace.

'Lord help, I don't know. Dooley, I reckon.'

'Dooley has better things to do than comb through tall grass lookin' for your teeth.' She went to the coatrack, took down her jacket, and sailed from the room, screen door slapping.

She was back in fifteen minutes. 'Hold out your hands,' she said to Harley.

Harley held out his hands.

She presented him with something wrapped in paper towel, then kissed him on the forehead and turned and went along the hall.

Harley's choppers.

Joy, he thought, noting the look of reprieve on Harley's face, was another sight to see.

'A wet knot stays tied longer'n a dry knot,' said Willie. He and Harley were having supper at Willie's house, out of the fray. 'My mother always said that. She was married in a pourin' rain that turned to hail by th' time they got th' horses home.'

'How long did it last?'

'Sixty years,' said Willie.

'Let's see. They's a fiddle, a bass, a guitar, a banjer, an' what else?' said Harley.

'Mandolin,' said Willie. 'An' a harmonica.'

'With all that t' play, they'll be some busy biscuits.'

There was a long silence.

'You gon' dance?' said Willie.

'I don't dance,' said Harley. 'Two left feet.'

'What if your girlfriend wants to dance?'

'Don't call her my girlfriend. Nossir, Miss Pringle is not a girlfriend and she don't look t' me like th' dancin' kind.'

'What are you wearin'?' said Willie.

'It's already laid out. Khakis, m' check shirt, lace-ups, m' good belt. How 'bout you?'

'Same, except I'm goin' with my plaid shirt. I've not wore my church shoes in a good while, they raise a blister. I'll have to go with my town shoes.'

'Are you gon' dance?'

'Nossir,' said Willie. 'I don't dance in front of people.'

'You dance by yourself?'

The two men laughed.

'You cackle like a layin' hen,' said Willie.

They were walking along the hay road at sunset, their boots kicking up red dust. Bowser and Bo followed—aimless, sniffing the weeds.

'All our dogs are old,' said Lace. 'All that wisdom and all those territorial rights—wouldn't that be hard for a puppy?'

'Hard for a little while, maybe. Then good.'

She was glad the Golden pup at the co-op had found a home. 'We need a puppy; I would love to have a puppy. But it's the wrong time.'

'Maybe it's the perfect time.'

She laughed. 'Are you crazy?'

He wouldn't want to answer that in the affirmative, but he'd always been a little crazy, and why stop now when he had just adopted the pup at the co-op? 'Bein' our animal doc,' Buster told him, 'you get first dibs.'

He took his cell phone from his jeans pocket. 'Dooley Kavanagh. Good evenin'.'

A single firefly in the tall grass; the last embers of the sunset. She watched his expression in the fading light.

'Yes,' he said. 'Of course. We'll be here for sure. We're ready. Great. Thanks.'

She heard it in his voice; this was what they had prayed for, worked for, waited for. Her heart was wild.

He spoke again briefly, put the phone in his pocket. 'It's happening,' he said.

'When?'

'Saturday.'

They stood in the narrow road, looking at each other, stunned.

'God help us,' she whispered.

'And he will,' said Dooley.

Ten

He drove into Mitford in Dooley's truck around nine a.m., through fog that flirted among the cedars and blew across the road in wisps.

'It's not fog, it's clouds,' one of his former parishioners liked to say, and that was of course true, for fog was merely a cloud that wasn't too smitten with itself to visit terra firma.

Harley would be coming to town in the afternoon, in his own truck. He hated the burning of extra gas, not to mention the spew of carbon monoxide into innocent mountain air. But it had to be done. Harley was toting twelve ten-gallon recycled paint buckets of well water, which he'd fill with armloads of Seven Sisters roses. The roses would overnight in the barn, and tomorrow morning would festoon a great deal of Meadowgate.

He let himself in their side door on Wisteria Lane and

heard the oddly consoling drone of Puny's vacuum cleaner above.

It had been a while since they lost Barnabas, but he never entered the house without being startled by his absence. 'Good boy,' he whispered.

And good smells. That would be Puny's lamb stew with plenty of garlic, and two peach pies for Monday's lunch with Henry and Walter and Katherine. Too bad that Puny and her brood couldn't attend the wedding; she had helped raise Dooley, after all. But there was an annual Cunningham family reunion, with attendants numbering a couple hundred.

He was grateful for the quietude of the study, the way the slipcover on the sofa seemed at home with itself, and noticed for the first time that his wing chair could use new upholstery. He would be happy to get back here tomorrow night with a brother and a first cousin and his cousin's wife. Family! All under one roof. While most people understandably took family for granted, he took it for grace.

And grandchildren one day, he thought, opening the spice drawer. But wait a minute. That wouldn't be happening. In view of the recent news, it was strange that his dogged yearning for grans had come circling back.

He crossed himself, gave thanks, and burgled their allspice, nutmeg, and cloves for his bakefest in the country. He also sought out a beef rub for the two tenderloins he had offered to roast. Why did he volunteer for doing this stuff? Truth be told, he was feeling a tad pressured.

'I guess you know,' said Lew Boyd when he went inside to pay his gas tab.

'Know what?'

'Gon' get a blow tonight.'

'Say that again?'

'Wind gusts up to sixty miles an hour. A blow. Tonight.'

Dear God. If they got such a thing, it would be a blow, all right.

'It's been on the news all mornin'.'

'We don't talk about weather in our house,' he said. 'Against the law.'

And there went his stomach roiling. The tent upside down in somebody's pasture, deviled eggs hither and yon. He would not mention this weather report to anybody at Meadowgate; he wouldn't even listen to the weather station on the drive home. No way did he want to know the particulars.

'Lord,' he said aloud as he switched on the ignition, 'may it please you to give us a wonderful day with good weather. That said, Lord—and I mean this sincerely—your will be done.'

There. He had dotted every *i* and crossed every *t*.

The orange marmalade cake sat on her kitchen counter in an open box.

Esther pointed to the contents with obvious satisfaction. 'Look in,' she said.

He looked in.

'*That*,' she said, 'is th' real deal. That is an *Esther Bolick* OMC. I've printed up a sign. It says Esther Bolick's Original OMC.' She handed over the sign, hand-lettered with a Sharpie on an 8x10 manila envelope.

'Says it all!'

'Then again, it doesn't say I'm th' one who actually made it.' She snatched the sign from his hand. 'Maybe it should say The Famous Original OMC Made by Esther Bolick *HER-SELF*. I do not want any confusion.'

'No, no, we certainly don't need any confusion.' As covertly as possible, he glanced at his watch. A lot of ground to cover. Plus he'd be working a five a.m. shift to get the hams done and the kitchen cleared for Lily and her crowd.

'Every Tom, Dick, and Harry in Mitford makes this cake,' she said. 'So th' sign should definitely be more specific about th' creator. What do you think?'

'Um,' he said.

'If Winnie wants to print up her own sign, that's fine by me. You need to mention that when you pick up from her place.' She closed the box, taped the lid shut. 'This is my weddin' gift to Dooley. He's a good boy. Not that I would be expected to give a gift.'

'Right. Certainly not. Very generous, Esther, but . . .'

'Or why don't you just stand by th' cake table and tell

everybody which is mine? You have more clout than a sign, people will believe you.' She stepped on the lever of her trash can and chucked the manila envelope.

'No, no. It would be redundant for me to stand by your cake and announce the name of its creator. The truth is, your cake will speak for itself.'

'Go on!' she said, shirking flattery. 'That's what Gene used to say.' Her eyes misted. It had been a brain tumor and a long goodbye.

He stooped a bit, leaned forward, and for emphasis removed his glasses. 'Your cake, Esther Bolick, will be recognized at once for its singular perfection, its precise placement of each and every orange slice, and when tasted, well—there will be no doubt whatsoever whose cake it is.'

And there was her sudden welcome smile.

'So thank you sincerely for your generous gift, but I already made out the check.' He pulled it from his shirt pocket, single folded.

'Tear it up!' she said, meaning it.

He carried the box to the truck and set it on the floor of the passenger side as carefully as if it were a grenade.

'Father!' Esther called from the porch.

'Yes, ma'am!'

'Tell 'em to slice it event-style!'

Event-style. He was afraid to ask. 'Will do!'

'An' run hot water on th' knife blade before you make each cut!'

He nodded, threw up his hand.

'If there's a crumb left on th' platter, I don't want to hear about it!' she hollered, grim as a troll.

'Listen to me, Esther! There will be fifty people at this wedding. There will *be no crumbs!*'

'And you leave it alone, you hear? No more comas out of you, Father!'

'Killer cake!' he shouted, and up he went into the refuge of the driver's seat and closed the door.

Driving away, he saw Esther in the side-view mirror, looking bereft. Though she didn't tell her age, she was up there—eightysomething, for sure—and definitely shriveled since he saw her at Christmas. In truth, he had done some shriveling of his own—he could look practically eye to eye with his wife, who, he was amused to learn, refused to shrivel. 'Wrinkle, maybe,' she said. 'But no shriveling.'

'The same forces that cause wrinkling cause shriveling,' he said, as if he knew.

She had given him a look. 'End of discussion.'

He peered again in the side-view mirror. Absolutely not. He couldn't do what he was suddenly inspired to do, he didn't have time. Time was of the essence. *No!*

He braked and shut off the engine and climbed out and sprinted up the driveway to the porch.

'Here's a hug,' he said.

'Why do I need a hug?'

'Why does anybody need a hug?'

And there was the smile again.

He drove to the Harpers', got no answer to his knock at the door, opened it and yelled, 'Anybody home?'

Hoppy came up the hall—wiry gray hair, wearing a pair of old green scrubs, looking his usual handsome and disheveled self.

'Olivia's out getting her mother-of-the-bride dress hemmed. You've done all the work while I've been totally immersed in flying medical personnel into three countries. I feel like a heel.'

They had a good embrace, complete with backslapping.

'Don't feel that way. I can't fly medical personnel anywhere, but I can weed-eat the north strip so you can get the better job done.'

'Thanks. Thanks. I owe you, Father. How's it going out there?'

'Consider it nailed,' he said, which was stretching the truth.

'Criminal,' Cynthia called his inability to kick back and let circumstances take their course. In his book, circumstances without close supervision had a tendency to wind up in the ditch. Actually, he'd be glad to come home to Mitford and let the young people get on with their lives.

'So fill me in,' said Hoppy. 'Let's go to the kitchen.'

'The barn is settled, the cattle are settled, the dress is settled. Now we're into what song they want for the first dance.'

Hoppy pulled out a couple of chairs at the kitchen table.

'Ours was "Come Rain or Come Shine." Have a seat. Remember that?'

He was pretty astonished that his former physician and parishioner literally burst into song.

'*I'm gonna love you like nobody's loved you*
Come rain or come shine . . .'

Hoppy laughed, mildly embarrassed. 'So do I qualify for the church choir?'

'You bet. I'm not sure I remember the song, but I'll never forget Miss Sadie's ballroom the night of your reception. A whole vast room done over just for you and Olivia. Musicians in formal attire. Angels painted on the ceiling. Food from the heavens. We'd never seen anything like it and never will again.'

He and Cynthia hadn't had a first dance. The reception had been held in the parish hall and yours truly had baked the ham and toasts had been delivered via a handheld mike that honked—and all the parish agog at their bachelor priest tying the knot with a good-looking woman.

Hoppy sang another line or two, as if to himself.

He'd never seen his old friend like this. Clearly, charitable work paid off in a marvelously unforeseen way.

Just as schoolteachers often had a pet—he had actually been one in seventh grade—he had Winnie Kendall.

When he walked into Sweet Stuff, there were the freckles, the amiable face anyone would be proud to wear, and the box open for inspection.

He peered in. 'Perfection, Winnie, perfection! I'd take a picture with my phone if I knew how.'

'Th' only thing I use my cell for is takin' orders.'

He started to peel off the bills.

'Put that back,' she said. 'This is my weddin' present.'

'You don't need to give a present.'

'You helped save my business, remember?'

'Please.' He proffered the money.

'I'm not takin' it.'

'Okay, be stubborn, and thanks a million. Lace and Dooley will appreciate it greatly, I assure you. This is a wedding on a shoestring.'

'There is no such thing as a weddin' on a shoestring, Father. Wait'll you total up th' damages.' There was a discreet pause. 'Have you seen Esther's little number yet?'

'Um.'

Winnie laughed. 'She's determined to outlive me and get her title back.'

The battle of the OMCs was up there with the Hatfields and the McCoys. Without shotguns, of course.

His two hams had made their way from the valley to the Local and he was excited about it.

Avis Packard was Mitford's grocer to three contiguous

counties, and the poet of comestibles. 'Free-range. Acorn fed. Moist and tender,' said Avis. 'In a nutshell . . . succulent!'

Bone-in, twenty-four pounds total. He hoisted the sack, grinning.

If there was a morsel left on the platters, he didn't want to hear about it.

He dumped his provender into the crew cab; he was heading home fully loaded.

'This simple little country weddin' has half killed several people,' Lily said yesterday.

'Amen,' he replied, not feeling especially liturgical.

He texted Mitford's local Realtor, Mule Skinner, and local newspaper editor, J. C. Hogan, barreled to the dry cleaner recently opened on the highway, and hit the door of Wanda's Feel Good Café at eleven-thirty on the nose.

'Two cakes in the car, temperature seventy-four and rising, no time to fool around,' he said to Wanda. 'Water, no ice. Turkey on whole wheat with tomato, no mayo.'

'You're no fun,' said Wanda.

'That's what they all say.' He would have his fun tomorrow at the potluck.

He skidded into his chair at the table.

'You heard th' weather news?' said J.C.

'Tent up, tables and rentals in the barn, porch covered, bourbon buried. All we can do. *C'est la vie.*'

J.C. wiped his face with a paper napkin. 'Can't you move it all inside? I mean, what can you do?'

'Pray, that's what we can do, have done, are doing, and will do. Out of our hands.'

'What was that about buryin' bourbon?' said Mule.

'A shameless superstition, otherwise known as a southern tradition, promoted by our farm help.'

'Why?'

He laughed. 'Don't ask.'

Wanda had arrived with the water pitcher. 'You gon' let it stay buried or you gon' dig it up?'

'Not my department.'

'I'd come help you dig it up, but I'm Baptist,' said Mule.

Wanda gave Mule a look. 'My sympathies.'

'What's new?' Omer Cunningham pulled out a chair.

'Big wedding out at Meadowgate. We're not invited,' said J.C.

'Family and friends,' he said. 'Small.'

Omer slapped him on the back. 'We've been hearin' about that. Congratulations, Father.' And there went Omer's smile, parading teeth as big as dimes. Omer was a decorated 'Nam vet and aviator who'd had a long span of bachelorhood but was now discreetly bronzed and happily married to Shirlene, who introduced spray tan to Mitford a few years back. This cosmetic amenity had never caught on locally, but the tourists were fond of it. 'It's paying for itself,' Shirlene had reported in a *Muse* interview in the business section, a single sheet printed both sides, two-color.

When was he going to talk about his brother coming? How was he going to introduce that news to people who had known him for years but had never heard of a brother?

'I'm sendin' Vanita out tomorrow to cover your big doings,' said J.C.

'No press,' he said.

'Come on. This is a big one. Everybody knows these kids, the whole town has been waiting for this wedding. Then there's Dooley's bull everybody's talkin' about. We'd like to get a shot of him, too.'

'No press, J.C. It's a small affair. Private.'

'Be a sport, buddyroe.'

He seemed doomed to occupy the compressed space between a rock and a hard place. 'That's not for me to decide. It would have helped if you'd brought it up earlier. It's a *family* wedding.'

'Mitford *is* family,' said J.C.

He felt like going home and digging up the bourbon himself.

June 13, 1:30 p.m.
    Waiting for the call. My stomach is in a knot.

Tommy called to say the Biscuits would be out between two and three tomorrow and Beth and her mom will fly into Holding this evening and rent a car. Her mom will stay in Wesley, but Beth will bunk with me and be my handmaid, as she says. She is so good~ I will owe her big-time for coming when things are so crazy at her office.

Sammy is flying in tonight from Minneapolis, where he just finished a big tournament, and will bunk in the library with the pool table~ the love of his life.

Sometimes I forget to breathe.

Olivia says our wedding present will be a surprise. I feel guilty for hoping it's a station wagon or hatchback~ my old Beemer is falling apart.

D truly loves me~ his love is more real to me every day. He says so a lot now. It's not just me anymore going I love you I love you. I am so insecure sometimes. I think he is a little scared about everything~ it's really enough to scare anybody. The wedding seemed super small when we started planning, but now it seems huge, even though it is the same number of people.

Tommy is so sweet and gifted~ and such a great friend to make the music happen for us. I wish he had somebody won-derful in his life. How do people find each other, Lord? I truly wonder. You put D and me in the same town with par-ents who are friends. That was easy, don't you think? But it seems hard for other people.

Here is really what I sat down to write~

I have been worried about doing my part to 'run' this place, God. And just yesterday, I started to believe I can. But only with your help.

Waiting for the call is the hardest. I almost told Cynthia this morning.

I love my dress.

He was speeding. Not a good plan.

The call had come from Dooley around two-thirty. Short, not much info, though what info there was was big. Very big. His heart did an A-fib number.

No surprise could be more disarming, no grace more be-nevolent.

Eleven

Jack Tyler was wearing a dark blue suit too large for his frame, with a dingy dress shirt and beat-up gym shoes. He carried his sole possessions in a black plastic bag with a tie—it appeared pretty empty—and held on tight to a stuffed kangaroo.

He had made it clear to the person who picked him up that he had to be called by his entire name. When people called him Jack, he felt like he was only half of himself, though he couldn't have explained this feeling.

He also let the person know that he hated this stupid suit. He had never worn such a thing before, it felt like a trap. He had begged to wear his jeans and favorite T-shirt but his granny made him wear this mess.

'That is a church suit from a church sale,' said his granny. 'They're church people over there. You need to make a good impression so they'll keep you around.'

He had lived with his granny in a trailer since he was a

baby, and now he was four. There had been room in the yard for his trike and her truck and that was it. There had been a sandbox, but somebody had backed over it with a dirt bike. If he rode his trike across a line that he could not see but that his granny talked about all the time, the dog next door went ballistic and he ran in the trailer and hid in the bathroom and shivered all over.

'There's a toy for you under the seat,' said the person.

'I don't want a toy.'

''Cause you already have a toy, right?'

'This is not a toy, okay?' His kangaroo was his friend. Roo was more real than the person driving this smelly bad truck.

When they turned into the driveway, he got a sinking feeling like he was going to upchuck. The person got out of the truck and came around to help him down.

'No,' he said.

He jumped down with his sack, remembering what his granny said. 'Maybe I'll come see you now an' again, but things is goin' on in my life, so don't look for me no time soon.'

'I won't,' he said.

This yard was big, the house was big, and this was more people than he had generally seen together at one time except when Sam Tully went off to heaven and people cried.

He wanted to cry, it felt like a cry coming, but his granny had said, 'Don't cry, you are not a baby, look at me, you don't see me cryin'. So he didn't cry, but he did think of climbing back in the truck when he saw the dogs, four of them, all barking straight at him but lying down. He had never seen a barking dog lying down.

He moved close to the person who had gone too fast around the curves. He had not said anything about going too fast but had held on to his kangaroo. His granny went fast, so he was used to going fast, except with somebody he did not know it seemed faster.

'There's your mom and dad right there, comin' out th' door,' said the person. 'Aren't they a pretty sight! We're late as th' dickens.

'It was th' log trucks!' the person shouted.

The mom and the dad were coming straight at him and the mom was crying even though she looked happy. He had never had a dad and could not remember anything about his real mom except the scar on her arm and the smell of her shampoo and her laugh, which was really loud. He made his body stiff just in case.

The new mom squatted down to his size. 'Hey, Jack Tyler,' she said. He stepped back. She was pretty like on TV and smelled like cookies.

The new dad squatted down. 'Welcome home, Jack Tyler.'

He could see straight into their eyes.

He hardly had any breath to ask the question. 'Does those dogs go ballistic?'

'Never,' said the dad. 'They are beyond ballistic.'

'Does they bite?'

'They don't have enough teeth to bite,' said the mom.

He thought of what his granny told him. 'You're jis' bein' fostered, you ain't adopted yet, so you be good, you hear?'

He thought he was pretty good except when he hated his granny so hard that he shivered and couldn't stop. He had run away once, but she caught him and took his kangaroo and throwed out the baby from the pouch. She had throwed it way out in the pond and he could not swim.

When he thought of that, he could not hold it back, so he cried now and they let him do it and they cried with him and the mom said it was okay.

He thought that maybe once in a while they could do it, anyway. 'Does they ever sometimes bite?'

'They don't have no teeth to bite,' said Harley. 'Like me. Looky here.' Harley made a toothless grin.

'For th' Lord's *sake!*' said Lily. 'Stop that! You'll scare 'im to death.'

He had never smelled so many good smells or seen so many people talking at the same time. On the table there was piles of cookies. Piles. He had never seen piles of cookies. And there was pies, too. A lot of pies.

'How about a sandwich with your lemonade?' said the mom.

No.

'With chicken and tomato and lettuce and mayo?'

No. He did not like to eat around strange people.

She handed him a cookie. 'It's chocolate chip,' she said. He thought her long hair was like on TV.

He took the cookie; it was still warm.

'Hey, buddy.'

It was somebody who looked like the dad but was another person with red hair. 'I'm Uncle Sammy.' Uncle Sammy was really tall and stooping down and holding out his hand. He could not shake it because he was holding his cookie.

'Welcome to th' z-zoo. We'll shoot us some pool after while,' said Uncle Sammy. 'Y-you okay with that?' he asked the mom. 'Abraham Lincoln shot pool, Mark Twain, President John Adams, V-Vanna White . . .'

She laughed. 'If there's time,' she said.

He had seen people on TV shoot pool.

'Who's your buddy there?'

'Roo.'

'He's losin' his stuffin'. I used to lose my stuffin' p-pretty regular.' Uncle Sammy laughed, rubbed him on his head just after the mom had combed his hair. 'Okay, Jack, be cool.'

'It's more than Jack,' he said. 'It's Jack Tyler.'

'Jack Tyler. G-got it. Goin' out to see th' cattle. Catch you later.'

He had drunk a whole glass of lemonade and besides, there were so many people he had to pee. He could not wait another minute and the dad was at the barn. 'I have to go,' he said to the mom.

'Do you want to leave your kangaroo here?'

'No,' he said.

She took him by the hand and led him to what she called the hall room and shut the door and he stuffed the cookie into his mouth. He saw lights behind his eyes. He had never tasted such a good cookie. It was soft and chewy and the chocolate was runny and he had to wipe his hands on the towel.

He did what had to be done and zipped up his church pants and stood for a long time wondering when it would be okay to go back out with all those people who seemed glad to see him and what he should do to not disappoint them and keep getting cookies.

He picked up Roo, made his body stiff just in case, and opened the door.

'Jack Tyler.'

He squatted before the boy, holding back the tears. What a holy amazement. 'Welcome home. I'm Dooley's dad, Father Tim.' Maybe that was too much information.

'What's that white thing around your neck?'

'My collar. I'm a priest.' Definitely too much information. 'Have you seen the cows?'

All the way home, he had wondered what to say to a four-year-old boy. It was a while since he'd been one.

The boy in the baggy suit was overwhelmed, as anyone would be. And he, the grown-up, had to search for words.

They looked at each other for a long moment. They were both pleading for something, though he couldn't say what. Perhaps the boy was pleading for someone to trust, and himself, a priest for a half century, pleading for a general forgiveness for not always knowing how to love. How he would get up from this squat was another matter.

'Here's a hug,' he said to Jack Tyler, who came without pretense into his arms. He held him close, feeling some of the tension flow out of the boy, out of the man, and grace flow in.

He walked with Dooley to the truck parked behind the corncrib and they climbed in and left the doors open.

'Two years ago, Lace and I went on a call with Hal. A pony with a bladder infection. There was a pond on the place, and when we drove out to the pony, we saw this little kid, maybe two years old, standing at the edge of the pond. He was squatting down and leaning over the water and we thought no way is this supposed to be happening. So Lace ran over to the little guy, he was in nothing but a diaper and it was plenty cold that morning. He said he was looking for something, so you can imagine where that was going.

'It was Jack Tyler. We both fell in love with him. Turns out his dad was killed in a motorcycle accident and his mother was long gone. He was living with his maternal grandmother, not a good thing. No way. We reported what we'd seen, but she was able to talk around the incident and keep him. We think it helped get her straight, but we worried, he stayed on our minds.

'We'd wanted to have kids when we got married. Four seemed to be the number. But we prayed about it and said, *Look, let's make it five, we need to get this little guy out of there.*

'I was two years away from graduating vet school, and the mother wouldn't relinquish rights, so it didn't look good. But we signed up anyway for fostering to adopt, and moved ahead, hoping.

'He's thoughtful and sensitive, Dad. You're going to love him.'

'Did this run through the court system?'

'It's a foster program by a home for kids like Jack Tyler. We did thirty hours of training, drove up on weekends to Meadowgate. There was a stack of homework, six sessions of five hours each with counselors, complete physicals—you name it, we did it, they totally worked us over. There were background checks and fingerprinting, plus house, fire, and environmental inspections.

'Because Lily and Willie would continue to work here, they were also interviewed and background-checked and so were the clinic staff. It was a hassle for everybody, especially Hal and Marge, but they were committed. We had to tell everything about our backgrounds, really emotional stuff. We hated it, there were times we wanted to give up. But we loved Jack Tyler, even though we weren't allowed to see him. We had to go on that one scenario by the pond.

'So we got the license, and we've been waiting for the call, waiting for the mother to relinquish all rights. We didn't know if that would happen, but it finally did. She gave him up, Dad.'

'Completely?'

'Completely. Living in California. Right now he's legally an orphan. No legal ties to anybody, he belongs to the state. We have to wait a minimum of six months before we can adopt.'

It was a lot, to say the very least, to take in. 'We'll be there for you, every way we can.'

'We wanted to tell you, but we didn't know if it was going to happen. Forgive us for not telling you. I tried a couple of times early on, but couldn't. I hate that I couldn't.'

'It's okay.' He regretted it, too, but any disappointment was completely overcome by one stunning reality:

He had a grandson.

He went searching for his wife, who was in the library with Olivia.

He and Cynthia held each other for a moment. Wonders never ceasing, joy without boundary.

She kissed his cheek. 'Have you seen him?'

'Just.'

He embraced Olivia, nearly speechless.

'We just realized we're grannies!' said Olivia.

Cynthia wore a mildly dazed look. 'I'm a *granny*! It seems only a couple of years ago I had acne.'

She and Olivia held hands and jumped around in a ragged circle.

'Oops,' said Cynthia. 'I forgot I can't jump around anymore.'

Olivia burst into laughter. 'Me, either!'

'I'm so happy to be your granny,' said the person squatting down. 'You could call me Granny Cynthy or maybe Granny C.'

'I already got a granny.' He had to tell people this because he could see they didn't know.

'And now you have two more,' said the mom. 'It's okay to have more than one granny. I promise.'

What would the new grannies do? His old granny had watched TV all day and all night with a lot of screaming and killing people. He hated screaming and killing people. His old granny made him eat his cereal dry and wear diapers till he was three. He had not liked anything about his granny, but he would not tell this to anyone ever. If she heard he had said something bad, she would come and scratch his eyes out. That's what she said she would do if he didn't shape up. He did not want his eyes scratched out; he wanted to see everything about his new life—for as long as it lasted.

Everybody was squatting down to talk to him. So he squatted down, too.

He really wanted to see the dad again; he was starting to forget what the dad looked like except for red hair. His real mom had red hair; he remembered that now.

A tall girl named Rebecca Jane squatted down and introduced herself and shook his hand. 'We are not real cousins,' she said. 'We're, like, faux cousins. Like, fake. But I think we should take cousins any way we can get 'em. I have a tree house I'm too old to play in if you'd like to come over and use it.'

'Jack Tyler! Look at you all dressed up. I'm Doc Owen. Great to have you on th' place.'

He looked way up at Doc Owen, who had big hands and a big voice and did not squat down. 'Just call me Uncle Doc. We'll go for a tractor ride when you get settled in, how about it?'

'Oh, looky here!' said Violet Flower. 'If you're not cute, ain't nobody cute. I don't suppose you'd stand up an' give me some sugar?'

He shook his head no and squeezed Roo really tight.

'Come,' said the mom, and took his hand.

'That was a circus,' said the mom.

They went to a door off the porch and she opened the

door and they went inside. There were two beds. One big and one little. A window was open; it was cool and dark in here. A table with a radio and stuff. And some clothes hanging and some shelves really high up with blankets and more stuff.

'This will be your bed tonight,' she said. 'You will sleep with . . .' They had talked at length with the counselor about this. They could wait and see what Jack Tyler decided to call them, or they could go ahead and set the standard themselves. They had no way of knowing whether this would work into what the counselors called a 'forever relationship,' but that's what she and Dooley wanted and believed in and were praying for, so why wait?

'You'll sleep with your dad.'

He nodded, dazed. It was like TV and not real. All the smells, the people shaking his hand and acting glad to see him, the dogs lying on the porch not going ballistic . . .

She sat on the side of the big bed and he sat on the side of the little bed.

'Tomorrow your dad and I are getting married. Do you know what that is?'

He didn't exactly know.

'We will be a husband and a wife. And you and your dad and I will share our lives right here on the farm with all the animals you're going to meet. We'll keep each other safe. We'll all be family.'

He tried to listen but could not. 'Are you on TV?'

'No. Why?'

He shrugged.

'You can call me Mom. If you'd like that.'

He hung his head and shrugged again.

'So let's put your bag on the bed now and your dad can put it on the shelf later. We have something for you.'

She got down on her hands and knees and pulled a box from under the little bed. She would save for later the toys the social worker said he would like—a wooden train and airplane, the cars—because right now, everything was too much.

'Would you like to open it?'

He sank to his knees, holding Roo, and she helped him get the tight lid off the first box.

Look!' she said. 'Jeans. And khakis. Even red plaid pants! Your dad picked those. And shirts. And pajamas. And . . .' She held up a new jacket. 'To match your eyes. Would you like to try it on? You can take off your suit jacket.'

'I hate this ol' stuff,' he said, ashamed, tearing off the suit jacket.

'We can put it in the church sale and you'll never see it again!'

He dropped the old jacket on the floor and she helped him put on the new jacket. She thought this was like having a layette for a boy no longer a baby.

'I think it looks great on you,' she said. 'What do you think? Does it feel good?'

He nodded yes. He couldn't imagine having so much stuff with tags on it.

'Tomorrow morning you can pick an outfit to wear to the family breakfast. And another outfit to wear when your dad and I get married.' She felt a kind of electrical current wink on inside when she used the M word.

She pulled out another box and sat back on her heels.

'May I hold Roo while you open it?'

'No,' he said, and fumbled the lid off with one hand.

He caught his breath. More than anything, he had always wanted boots.

He looked at her without meaning to and saw the expression on her face, the way she was looking at him, and thought he should say something but he didn't know what it should be. It was like there was a huge fight going on inside him. He wanted to lie down on the little bed and curl up and cry and cry and cry and at the same time he wanted to run and run and run and holler and laugh really hard. And hug the mom.

'These boots is tight.'

'They'll break in,' said the dad. 'It takes a little time. They're actually a half size bigger. You'll grow into 'em before you know it.'

They had walked out to see the chickens and take a look at the cattle.

'See out there at the tree line? Five heifers. Red Angus.'

He had watched *Sesame Street* when his granny was asleep

and could count pretty good. 'One, two, three, five, six. I mean four, five.'

'Good job! Whoa, look comin' here, Jack Tyler.'

He backed away from the fence.

'It's okay. Stand close to me.' The dad touched him on the shoulder and he stood close to the fence again and close to the dad's leg, but his heart was beating fast.

'This is Choo-Choo. Choo-Choo, this is Jack Tyler.'

It was big as a trailer, big as a building, big as a mountain, and was looking straight at him, flicking its tail.

'You must never go inside the fence, okay? Never. This is a big bull and most any bull can be very dangerous. Okay?'

'Okay.'

'You know what dangerous means?'

'Yeah.'

'Never stick your hand through the fence to pet him. Also very dangerous. Okay?'

'Okay.' He would never stick his hand through the fence to pet this scary huge monster.

'Look at the musculature,' said the dad. 'The way he's designed. The poise in this enormous creature is phenomenal.'

There was a happy look on the dad's face as the bull lowered its huge head.

'Man!' said the dad.

He watched the dad for a time, then stood up as tall as he could in his new jeans and new blue shirt and new boots, and looked at the bull with long eyelashes eating grass.

'Man!' said Jack Tyler.

He was heading up to pack for the trip back to Mitford tomorrow night.

At the foot of the stairs, Sammy gave a shout from the library, where he and Jack Tyler were shooting pool.

'Call us butter,' said Sammy, ''cause we're on a roll!'

D and I are in love~ with Jack Tyler. ☺

*After our walk-through, JT ate his supper as if starved,
had a bath and put on his new pajamas. He is truly precious
with a tender spirit. D and I tucked him into bed and prayed
for him and I thought I would read to him but that would be
a story about other people and places. We decided he might
like to know about the people and places that belong to him
now so he can begin a story all his own.*

*So D and I told him about his grandpas and grannies
and the attic room where he can play on rainy days and how
he has lots of uncles and aunts and barn cats and guineas
and one day maybe llamas and he was asleep while we were
still talking~ foundered by dread and wonder and strangers
and pizza.*

*I cannot believe how all this makes me feel, the bigness of
it in my heart. Dooley went to sleep too while I was telling the
story but woke up when Sammy and Harley came looking for
him to shoot a game of eight ball. I guess that was the bach-*

elor party! I am so excited, Lord, and so exhausted and thankful and goofy. Beth is on her way, should be here any minute. Tomorrow everything will change and stay the same, all at once.

'. . . believe in a love that is being stored up for you like an inheritance, and have faith that in this love there is a strength and a blessing so large that you can travel as far as you wish without having to step outside it.'

Rmr

'It's scary to think of being a wife and a mother all at once,' said Lace. She had finished blow-drying her hair and was in her pj bottoms and the faded T-shirt that said *Love Is an Act of Endless Forgiveness.*

'I've read all the training stuff they gave us, but it can't tell you everything. I hope I never let Jack Tyler down in some terrible way. I'll be flying by the seat of my pants; I hope people won't be disappointed in how I do it.'

'Just be who you are,' said Beth, 'because those who mind don't matter and those who matter don't mind.'

'Who said that?'

Beth laughed her ironic laugh. 'Adapted from Dr. Seuss. So what's in the bridal bouquet?'

'Seven Sisters roses, stephanotis, and kale.'

'*Kale?*'

'Because it's sort of crisp and ready for anything.'

'I never knew that about kale. You're biting your nails.'

She had tried so hard to stop doing that. Gloves maybe would work.

'We all have a big breakfast together in the kitchen around ten—Father Tim's brother Henry is coming up from Charlotte in the morning with Harley. There'll be sixteen or seventeen of us. And the musicians will be here at two and you can rehearse. Then we'll have a walk-through of the ceremony with everyone. I'm thinking that before I get dressed, I'll take Dooley over to the clinic to see his wedding present. Just the two of us, we've hardly had five minutes together in days.'

'He'll be blown away. Who will ever again be given such a fabulous, fabulous present?'

She hadn't mentioned the possibility of big winds. She went to the window and opened it. Clouds racing. Moon full.

Breezy.

'I want to remember everything,' she said, closing the window. 'Pray that I can remember everything.'

'Breathe,' said Beth. 'It helps.'

They turned down the covers—eleven-thirty—turned off the lamps, and got into bed.

'How did you feel?' said Lace. 'I remember you seemed so poised, so collected, even though Freddie was late.'

'I was not poised and not collected. You know how I have this armor plate that I use way too much. I'll love singing your love song tomorrow because I never felt that way about anybody ever. Freddie was crazy, but I was way crazier to marry him. There were red flags all over the place. God tried to tell me, my parents tried to tell me, you tried to tell me. But no, Freddie and I went out there and wreaked havoc.

'I look at your beautiful, simple, recycled dress and think how selfish I was to ask for a dress that cost more than my dad's first car. My sweet dad, I spent the rest of his life making that dress up to him, though he found it hilarious that I sold it on eBay. He was such a sweet guy. Mom and I miss him every day. Your dad is a sweetie, too, and your mom, and Dooley's parents. We are so blessed, Lace Face.'

'Thanks for being my best friend ever,' said Lace. 'I'll sing at your wedding.'

'You can't sing!' said Beth.

'True,' she said. 'But for you, I would try.'

Twelve

Everybody was asleep.

'Everybody except me, James Herriot, creeping sore and
exhausted towards another spell of hard labor.

'Why . . . had I ever decided to become a country vet? I must
have been crazy to pick a job where you worked seven days a week
and through the night as well. Sometimes I felt as though the practice was a malignant, living entity; testing me, trying me out, putting the pressure on more and more . . .'

Everybody was asleep here, too, all but the country vet.
At two in the morning, he'd waked up in the bed where he
always slept at Meadowgate and heard the wind. He lay facing the wall, reading the handwritten James Herriot quote
illumined by the full moon.

Hal had given the quote to him years ago, as a reminder
to carefully evaluate any notion of mixed practice. He had
pinned it to the wall, done the evaluation, and chosen to
work with small animals. But . . .

One of the basic principles in raising cattle was to know they're creatures of habit and obsessive about food. They would brook no slack for the frivolities of a wedding—he'd have to get out there early with the grain. The heifers were on a growth plan of several pounds a day and the pastures weren't yet improved enough to get the job done without grain. Maybe he'd check them one more time before the ceremony . . .

He closed his eyes and turned over.

They had known weather was moving in but, obeying some unspoken house rule, had resisted talking about it. All except Willie, who had pulled him aside, urgent. Gusts up to sixty miles per hour. Okay, so they got everything even more safely under cover and checked with the tent guys—they would be willing to come out and take it down but couldn't come back on Sunday and put it up again. In any case, rest assured that they had laid on extra guy wires and anchors, and given the probability of a north wind, the tent would be somewhat protected by the stand of trees across the road. Which was, in his opinion, stretching it.

He and Willie and Harley and Lace had turned the stacked chairs on their sides beneath the shed, set the rental crates in the center of the barn aisle, and stuck the buckets of roses in the middle stall. As for the cattle, they would hunker down at the tree line—not the best place in high winds, but that's what cattle do.

He opened his eyes.

His heart kicked, then did a racing beat. How could he have forgotten? He sat up, startled.

Jack Tyler! Right here beside him on the cot.

In the light of the moon, he looked to see whether the boy was breathing. Yes. Steady. Jack Tyler was out cold from the hard business of being passed from one hand to another.

He was somehow stunned by the flesh-and-blood reality of the small figure in this small room. Knowing for two years that this could happen was no help in making it visceral knowledge.

He was a dad. This had not sunk in when they signed the papers or when Jack Tyler climbed down from the truck, or even when he and Lace put him to bed with a story and a prayer. Now, in the early hours of their wedding day, it was striking home.

There were so many game changers hitting at the same time. No trickle, no steady stream, just a gusher. He could be overwhelmed and zone through his wedding and the actuality of the boy who would one day be their legal son, or he could breathe deep and take it all in.

He probably shouldn't have opted for the pup. But it was act fast or lose her, and she was exactly what Lace wanted, what they both wanted, what Jack Tyler would surely be thrilled to have as a buddy. What was done was done; the eight-month-old Golden was in her crate at the clinic and no looking back.

He got out of bed and cranked open the window to the

oncoming scent of rain. The wind was definitely up. Clouds raced across the moon, light was quickly gone.

He closed the window and stood by the small bed for what seemed a long time.

It's said that a low-pressure system is a good influence on sleep. Leaves curl up, dogs lie splayed on porches, people do less tossing and turning and tend to snooze, if permitted such feckless behavior, up to two hours longer than average.

From a profound slumber, he was suddenly awake.

He turned on his side, facing his sleeping wife. The mattress seemed to shudder again—something like the coin-operated 'massage mattress' offered long ago in a Jackson hotel.

Wind.

A turn-of-the-last-century wood-shingled farmhouse could seem pretty cozy in rain or snow, but fragile as paper in a harrying wind that banged the occasional shutter. He heard the keening sound so beloved of the horror movie, then a muffled boom he identified as if by clairvoyance—he sat up. A tree had gone down.

He eased out of bed and dressed by the light of his cell phone and pulled on his work boots.

In a rain so warm it felt tropical, they took what inventory they could with flashlights and lanterns.

One tree down.

One barn shed roof partially demolished by the fallen tree.

Forty-two dinner plates and as many glasses smashed in their crates.

A few heavy limbs from the pin oaks gouged into the rear lawn.

Power off.

On the other hand:

Dogs safe, cats safe, chickens and guineas safe.

Dooley had already been out to the field. Cattle safe.

House safe, clinic safe, vehicles unharmed, not to mention the benediction of rain for the fields, and the creek running bold. As for the tent, it had not been blown to Kentucky. It stood trim, with but a wet leaf or two plastered to the canvas.

A few epithets, considerable headshaking. 'That bourbon ain't completely workin',' said Harley.

He and Dooley and Sammy and Willie and Harley would dry off, turn back into their beds, and meet for the cleanup at seven.

Power back on. Rain gone. Five-fifteen a.m., and he was sleep-walking around the kitchen.

'Plenty of pepper,' Avis had said of the tenderloin prep. 'Rub it in. Cracked, not ground. And rosemary. No way can you leave out th' rosemary.' On and on, Avis had gone, like a parakeet in full throttle—the wine pairing, the pink center, the blast-furnace oven to begin . . .

If they'd had just one more day to get ready . . .

'Buck up,' he sermonized himself. 'Look how many days we've just had. Forty-two, give or take! Always after something more, us humans. Always after something more.'

She went a few minutes before seven to the room off the porch. Dooley was up and dressed and drinking coffee in the kitchen. Jack Tyler was sleeping, he said.

But Jack Tyler was awake and agitated.

'Roo is gone!' he wailed.

'Look under your blanket,' she said, stooping over the bed.

'No, Roo is gone!'

The sobbing, the utter despair.

'But look! Here's Roo on the floor. Right here. He must have fallen out of bed last night.'

She handed him the unstuffed toy and sat beside him and held him and wiped his eyes with the tail of her shirt. 'Time to wash your face and get dressed.'

He didn't wash his face at his granny's. 'Why?' he wailed.

'Because this is the day!'

'What day?'

'When you walk down the aisle behind Aunt Beth, carrying the pillow with the rings. Like we did yesterday evening.' They had put together a mini walk-through so he wouldn't be plunged without knowing into the big walk-through fol-

lowed closely by the real thing. They had tried to keep it light
and fun, but it been too much for him.

'I don't want to,' said Jack Tyler. He had dropped the ring
pillow in the grass and gone stiff all over and couldn't move.
Everything around him felt lost and big. He hadn't known
whether to pick up the pillow and keep going or run and hide
forever. The mom had hugged him and said it was okay and
he was flooded with shame for not doing it right.

She felt his wild alarm. The terrible timing of it . . . but
no, it wasn't terrible timing, it was God's timing and it was
perfect, God knew everything there was to know about four-
year-old boys. She needed to remember this every step of the
way, one step at a time.

'You don't have to do it. It's okay.' She tousled his hair,
dark as mahogany with a glimmer of red in the morning
light.

How could he say this? 'I want to walk with you.'

'I'll be walking with Granpa Hoppy.' We cannot have everything in this life, she thought, not even when we are four.
'So I know it's hard to carry a pillow with rings on it and
carry Roo, also. Could Granny O hold Roo?'

'No,' he said.

She breathed out, breathed in. A bird sang outside the
open window.

'I have a great idea,' he said, solemn as rain.

An idea! Yes!

'You can carry Roo. And I can walk with you an' carry
th' pillow.'

'Ah.' This was head-spinning. 'But I'll be carrying flowers and holding Granpa Hoppy's arm.'

He looked up, tears still shining in hazel eyes flecked with gold. 'Only you can hold Roo,' he said.

It was every hand on deck, save for Cynthia and the bride and her handmaiden.

Cynthia took Jack Tyler to join the work crew, but he was to stand out of the way at all times, did he understand that? He nodded yes.

The first order of business was to clean up the broken glass and china. Cynthia was to get on the phone to Marge and Olivia and the Flower Girls and ask them to bring whatever plates and glasses could be spared. As Harley was on the road to Charlotte to fetch Henry, there was no one to run to Mitford and divest the Kavanagh cupboards of china and glassware.

Mink Hershell arrived with his chainsaw and a newer-model tractor, using the rear entrance in order to avoid tracks in front of the barn. They heaved the old maple off the shed roof and dropped it on the ground to be sawed into firewood and seasoned under cover. It would warm thrice, similar to Thoreau's observation, those who brought it down, cut it into logs, and took pleasure from the fire.

In the morning light, the astonishing shallowness of its

root system was exposed for the first time to human view. Indeed, the root ball, so easily plucked up by wind, was a depository of artifacts.

Dooley hefted Jack Tyler onto his shoulders so he could see the Cheerwine bottle cap lodged in the dirt near a taproot.

Over here was a hand-wrought nail most likely used for shoeing a horse.

And there, a shard of blue and white pottery—all of it proclaiming those gone before us, the communion of saints.

Jack Tyler wanted the shard and was allowed to dig it out with his own hands. He would wash it and keep it, he said, and be careful not to cut himself on it.

A thorough exam of the shed structure discovered it stable enough for merrymaking. And though the tree removal had been a muddy piece of business, Willie put a shine on things. The rain had stopped around three-thirty, he said, and the forecast for today was seventy-two degrees with sunny skies. Meaning that by afternoon, the moisture would be wicked away with the same haste it had come, leaving them as dry as Ezekiel's bones.

High five.

A storm in the middle of the night. Beth and I slept through it and so did Jack Tyler. Limbs all stacked in one spot in the

yard and the tree taken off the shed roof. Thank you, God, for everything!

The wedding program we printed two weeks ago at the clinic does not have Jack Tyler's name in it. He is willing to be the ring bearer but only under certain conditions! He cried this morning but is a truly brave boy~ so thoughtful and re-strained. D says he will give JT a chance to 'fly apart' to-morrow in case he needs to. Just added JT's name and Amanda will run off the copies. Bumps in the road! Glad we did not set the wedding time for morning as first planned ages ago.

Note: We decided to add five words to the vows, the words Dooley's granpa used to say to him. And the proces-sional hymn was Miss Sadie's favorite. We love remembering them.

Our family motto, decided today:

A cord of three strands is not quickly broken. Ecclesi-astes 4:12

Henry Winchester had never been to North Carolina. He had spent his adult life traveling the rails from New Orleans to Chicago and back again.

There had been no other world, nor had he ever wanted any other than the rocking and creaking and gliding of the train. It was a womb, a cradle, all that and more, and the years spent working his way along the corporate ladder had been infinitely pleasing and endlessly absorbing. He had managed to love all of it, perhaps especially those long-ago last days of the sleeping-car porters. During the few months he was a proud member of the brotherhood, he had never minded being called George a time or two; he was proud of a designation born out of ignorance but resonant with the imperial riches of men who had stood up and been counted and changed things forever.

On the train from Birmingham to Charlotte, he had traveled a pretty flat bed, and now this magnificent countryside with the world's oldest mountains—hard to believe as that may seem—right outside the window of this truck. Compared with the upstart juveniles of, say, the Alps or Everest, the Blue Ridge mountains were worn to a nub. In these elders was some divine wisdom he might have picked out like a walnut from its shell if he had more time.

But here was this good driver with what's called 'a lead foot,' this slightly built man with as strange a speech as any in Mississippi, albeit a far more rapid kind of speaking which his adoptive school-principal father would have enjoyed immensely. 'It's what they call hillbilly talk,' Harley Welch said in good humor.

They were riding on something called the Parkway, a world that, but for Timothy, he would never have seen. He was astonished that such a land existed, though he knew in his head that it did; he'd seen it in the pages of *National Geo-*

graphic, his favorite reading material. This landscape spoke to him in a private and oddly familiar way—it was fearsome and consoling at the same time, like life itself.

Joy springs all radiant in my breast, he thought, limning a line of Dunbar. *'Tis wealth enough of joy for me / in summer time to simply be.*

With his mother gaining on ninety-seven years and his own vigor unpredictable, he wasn't likely to come this way again.

But he was glad he came this time, oh yes, and thank God and Brother Timothy for the good health to do it.

He managed a thirty-minute nap and rummaged through the contents of his sock drawer, now in a grocery bag to be loaded into Cynthia's car. He needed a handkerchief and here it was, clean but unironed—this was not a household for ironing handkerchiefs.

It had been six or seven years since that long patch in Memphis by Henry's hospital bed. The doctors had removed stem cells from his bloodstream and conducted them into Henry's. The chances of a match between half brothers had been less than five percent. Yet he and Henry, his junior by a decade, had won the lottery, a triumph that dosed them and the medical staff with gratitude and astonishment.

He looked out the window of the bedroom and saw the

truck pulling in. Harley had judged the drive time almost to the minute.

His heart hammered as he raced downstairs. 'It's Henry!' he called to whoever was listening as he blew past the kitchen and out to the glider porch.

Henry was stepping down from the truck, looking the tall, refined gentleman that he assuredly was, and more like their father than he remembered.

My God. Henry. Here!

The tears came freely for both as he embraced the man whose heart pumped Kavanagh blood to the full extent of his own. There was the backslapping, the shy embarrassment of open feeling, and they stood away then and pulled out their handkerchiefs at precisely the same moment.

They looked with wonder at their similar white squares, one monogrammed with *W*, one with *K*, but nothing fancy.

'Value pack,' he told Henry, and they wiped their eyes and laughed. A good, deep, relieving laugh.

There was Lace's dad wheeling into the driveway in his ancient Volvo, windows down as usual.

Dooley threw up his hand as he walked out to the car. 'Hey, Doc!'

They did a high five through the open window.

His soon-to-be father-in-law grinned. 'Hey, Doc yourself.'

'DPAW,' whispered the Clergy Spouse.

This was code for Don't Pray Around the World, and short for Do Not Let This Hot Breakfast Get Cold.

Whenever he was headed into a big occasion with full vestments—and bless her heart, she couldn't help it—his wife suddenly became higher and mightier than her usual self, dispensing directives of every stripe. But how could he not pray around the world, as it were? How could he not? Look at this bountiful table, at the people God had joined together out of the seeming blue. Look at the weather, the minor miracle of *that*.

He was somewhat breathless as he held the chair for Lace and for once was nearly speechless. He had not prepped for this giving of thanks and praise and felt oddly small, as if, in accordance with Absalom Greer's old saying, he could crawl under a snake's belly wearing a top hat.

He had prayed in cathedrals and at the bedsides of two or three bishops, but never with more to give thanks for than this day, in this generous place where they were celebrating a marriage, a child, a new home, family ties, a new business, the completion of academic studies, and of course all those further, though often unseen, blessings bestowed by Almighty God made known through Jesus Christ.

He sat and spread his napkin across his lap and looked down the kitchen table.

At the far end, Lace to Dooley's left, Jack Tyler on the right—a family formed overnight.

And there was Sammy looking confident and sort of streamlined, you might say, what with his cable TV pool-shooting competitions, and Harley and Willie and Marge and Hal and Rebecca Jane and his amusing and upbeat Clergy Spouse and Jessie, Dooley's teenage baby sister, next to her brother Pooh with the familial crop of red hair, and Beth, Lace's college friend and financial guru, and her mother Mary Ellen, an attractive fiftysomething widow, and then Hoppy Harper, his former physician and parishioner who could have been a stand-in for Walter Pidgeon, next to the lovely Olivia Harper, and at his right, Henry. Olivia and Henry, each delivered from certain death—one with a new heart, the other with new stem cells.

And now everyone holding hands and forming the small but mighty link that was its own bread.

'Almighty God.' He cleared his throat, concerned that he may choke up. Then again, how could he not?

Violet Flower took the hanging clothes off the rod and folded them over her arm. Dooley was neat, which was a good thing. Counting the box of Jack Tyler's new clothes, and his ragged jeans and T-shirt, which were now washed and folded, she could do this in three trips.

It had taken four trips for Lace's pile. It would all go in

the big master bedroom closet, which Father Tim and Cynthia just about emptied last night and loaded in their car. Boy, if this wadn't musical chairs.

She liked deciding how to hang clothes. She did not do the military-type routine of all blue together, all green together, whatever. That was anal. She just did a basic all shirts, all jackets, all pants together for men, and all dresses, all skirts, all pants and blouses together for women. What wadn't hangin', she would fold and put on the shelf—Lace on th' left, Dooley on th' right.

She checked her watch: ten-fifteen on the dot. She needed to get this project done by eleven, when breakfast would wrap up and the house would be crawling with people. She knew what to leave behind for Dooley and Lace and Jack Tyler getting dressed for the Big Knot. During the dancing, she would haul the leftover stuff to their rooms, where it would all be ready for their new life. She would not charge her time for this; it would be her present to the bride and groom.

She made her way up the back stairs. It would be easy doin' Jack Tyler's little room, which was right next door to Lace and Dooley's. She would cut off the tags and hang up the clothes from the big box, and that would be the end of it for now, bless his heart. He was a serious young'un an' cute as a bug's ear, she could eat him with a spoon.

The whole house smelled like ham and roast beef and cookies and cheese wafers and breakfast casserole. Her mama did not care for food odors, she would be pumpin' that can of Lavender Field Supreme till she got corporal tunnel.

She liked the look of Dooley's good denim jacket and jeans next to Lace's red-print dress with th' ruffled hem. Totally romantic. Hangin' smack in the center of th' rod, which would be th' dividin' line, the dress and jeans outfit looked like a couple dancin'.

She remembered starting a new life with her sweetie. Before she could hang one scrap of Lloyd Goodnight's pitiful wardrobe in her closet, she had to wash it, starch it, iron it, sew on buttons, whatever. He was a brick mason, for heaven's sake; he did not have clean, sporty clothes.

She remembered hanging his good plaid shirt and dress pants next to her best cowgirl outfit, which she wore for singing at parties. 'What a good-lookin' couple!' she had said of the duo that looked almost as sexy as the real thing.

In the library, Sammy Barlowe was doing a demo, something like the stuff he did on cable TV. He was totally in the big time, but not the *big* big time. Not yet. He was working on it twenty-four/seven and found that he really liked teaching other people how to do it, though he was not teaching any of his private tricks, they would stay private.

It was best to start young, he thought, which was the way a lot of great shooters started. He'd made his first shot at the age of nine—or was it eight?—in the ball hall in Holding. He had heard the crack of cue tip against resin a million times, but when his own tip smacked the ball, he got a feeling he'd never forget and couldn't explain but which he kept looking to have again. 'It's like your first time with a girl,' a shooter in Illinois had said. 'You ain't ever goin' that way again.'

He had swept out the place in Holding and emptied ashtrays and hauled out the stinking garbage in return for his table fees. He had been tall for his age but still too short to get good leverage, so he dragged a Cheerwine crate around the table and stood on it and had taken a lot of crap for doing it. But the crate got the job done, and eventually he totally hammered the goons who messed with him.

This little squeak, Jack Tyler, was smart. He had him kneeling in a kitchen chair and handling the smallest stick in the house, while Doc Owen worked the biggest stick in the house, given hands the size of a baseball mitt. He wished he had his Frank Paradise cue to show everybody, but no way did he ever travel with that; it was a museum piece and how he came to own it was like a miracle, if there was such a thing. He was reminded that Father Tim and Father Brad said miracles happen all the time.

Father Brad would be here today. He'd like seeing the guy who made him hang off the side of a cliff looking down two thousand feet with a nosebleed and climb a mountain that seemed like freaking Everest and sleep in a snow tent. No way would he ever do that stuff again, even though he had loved it and still talked about it a lot. It was the snow tent that did it. He didn't just think he was going to freeze and die, he knew freaking well he was going to freeze and die. And then the thing with God happened . . .

He was at home around a pool table. Anchored. He could be coming apart, but let him walk into a room with a great table and he would, like, exhale, and breathe again. Not once since he got here had he wanted to be like Dooley or felt jealous of what Dooley had. That old stuff was over. Dooley was Dooley, he was Sammy. Being Sammy was enough. Sometimes it was too much. Like, Hey, God, can you drive, I am runnin' this thing in th' ditch.

He liked that a little crowd was buzzing around. His old buddy Harley was standing by with a big grin and Doc Harper with his Nikon was shooting everything that moved and there was ol' Pooh with his mouth still hanging open from the last shot and Jessie stuck over in the corner—he didn't have a clue about the nose rings—and people he didn't know, like a woman with long gray hair who kept staring at him. They were all kind of quiet and respectful of the demo instead of blabbing the whole time.

The musicians were tuning up out there, the sound pumped in through the open window. Banjo, he liked th' banjo, and a harmonica . . .

He thought the kid was cooler than Doc Owen, who was laughing and joking around and not being serious about it, but Jack Tyler was dead serious and wanted to learn whatever was going down.

'Like this,' said Sammy, hunkering over the table with his cue.

He saw that his brother was traveling like the pros—with a rolling one-suiter, now parked in the hall.

Henry removed an envelope from a zippered side pocket. 'Mama sent you something.'

Peggy. The one he'd run to with his skint knee, cut jaw, bashed nose, and broken heart—a second mother. Peggy had disappeared from the Kavanagh household when he was ten. Vanished. Somewhere in his soul he had searched for her for decades. And then he had found her—and Henry.

He opened the envelope and withdrew a sallow piece of paper, folded twice and hard-worn.

> *It was me*
> *Who ate your pie.*
> *I am sorry.*
> *Timothy*
> *Age 7*

'When Mama left, she carried that with her, it meant a lot. You had gone in her little house while she was working and ate her last piece of pie.'

'Pumpkin!' he said. Back it came from the vortex of memory that would scarcely disclose what he had for breakfast.

'Your mother made you write it.' Henry was smiling, a light in his eyes. 'Mama said you were left-handed when you wrote it. They started training you to your right soon after, she said. That's what they did back then.'

Words he'd written seven decades ago had come home. He shook his head, full of wonder: 'Will the circle be un-broken?'

Henry smiled. 'By an' by. But not yet. Not yet.'

The woman with long gray hair was among the last to leave the library.

'I enjoyed watching you work,' she said.

He thought she seemed sort of nervous. 'Thanks. You shoot pool?'

'No,' she said, 'but my son does.'

'Is he any good?'

'The best.'

'Great. It's a good game. Winston Churchill shot pool.' He was always trying to get people to understand that pool wasn't all about loafing and drinking and gambling and spit-ting. Important people did it and he wouldn't mind being important but mostly he hoped one day to be inducted into the Hall of Fame. That was his dream.

'And Martin Luther King and Babe Ruth,' said the woman.

'Yes, ma'am!' He laid his stick in the case Father Tim gave him a few years ago, and snapped it shut.

'I saw a video of Mr. Orbach playing a nine ball with Ms. Laurance,' she said. 'On TV.'

He thought the woman was very cool to know about Ewa Laurance and Jerry Orbach.

Beth emerged from a shower in the minuscule bathroom, her wet hair wrapped in a towel. 'So tell me about the way he walks,' said Beth.

'Who?'

'Tommy. I was worried about doing the wedding song with a harmonica—I mean, really! But he promised it would work and it actually does; it gave me chills with that great sound system he just bought. He's an amazing musician.'

'So his leg got pretty broken up from the knee down,' said Lace, 'when he and Dooley were—maybe twelve? Miss Sadie's Hope House was under construction. The man running the job is now Dooley's stepdad. He told Dooley to never go on the job site after hours. It was pretty well known that the job site was taboo. But Dooley wanted to go and asked Tommy to go with him and they were fooling around on a big pile of lumber. Dooley had a chance to jump off the pile before it came apart, but Tommy didn't.

'It took a long time for his bones to heal. Now he sort of walks like a cowboy, somebody said. Dooley really struggled with this for years, he blamed himself, but Tommy said he was totally up for doing it, that Dooley was not responsible at all. You know Dooley had to take care of his little brothers and sister for days at a time. He had to grow up fast, and when something went wrong, he blamed himself. He still does that.'

Beth turned the blow-dryer on high, combing her short blond hair with her fingers. 'He is really, really cute.'

'I know. I'm so lucky.'

Beth laughed. 'I was talking about Tommy.' She sat on the side of the bed. 'And his voice. I don't know much about country music, but don't you think he's sort of special?'

'I do, we love him. But he's really unpolished for a Yankee girl with a family who owns railroads and works at Goldman Sachs.'

'That was my great-great-grandfather who owned railroads; we're all poor as church mice now. And trust me, it's no big deal that I'm at Goldman.'

'But it was always your dream to work there.'

'Maybe it isn't my dream anymore.'

'Tell me.'

Beth shrugged, turned off the blow-dryer, walked to the window. 'It doesn't matter.'

'Of course it matters.'

'Wow. My mom and Father Brad.'

'Doing what?'

'Standing by the fence together. She's giving him such a smile. I haven't seen her really smile in a long time. Who is Father Brad, anyway? Is he okay?'

'He was our premarital counselor and one of the big reasons Sammy made a turnaround. Sammy did Father Brad's annual boot camp for teens—hiking, mountain climbing, snow camping, praying—it was super intense. It took three boot camps for Sammy.'

Beth was pressing her nose against the glass to get a better look. 'I mean, he's sort of a hunk for a priest. Is he a nice person? He had better be a nice person.'

Lace laughed. 'They're just standing by the fence together, right? And yes, he's a completely wonderful person.'

They were ducking out to the clinic together, hand in hand like kids running away from home. And there was Danny Hershell and his kid brother tying cans to the rear bumper of Dooley's truck, which now displayed a hand-lettered sign: *Just Married.*

'Hey, dude,' said Dooley, 'we appreciate it, but we're not goin' anywhere.'

Danny Hershell was pretty devastated.

'But keep doin' what you're doin', okay? And thanks. We'll drive it around tomorrow and honk th' horn at your place.'

The music and walk-through, sans dogs, had gone smoothly, with a lot of laughter. Jack Tyler was fine with everything and she was relieved. Relieved too that she could still be in her old jeans and a farm shirt for this stolen time with Dooley.

He unlocked the rear door. 'After today, you're going to be stuck with me,' he said.

'I've waited years to be stuck with you.'

They stepped inside; he held her tight against his heart, his flesh and bones.

'I want to sleep with you forever,' she said.

'I want to sleep with you forever back. I love you. I need you, I thank God for you.'

She leaned into the sinew of his frame, where she always learned something new, and they held each other.

They went along the hall then to the recovery room, where patients slept or stared out of their crates longing for home.

'Look!' she said, dismayed. 'It's Homer.'

Homer lay on a blanket, an IV needle in his left ear. He opened one eye and gazed at her.

'You didn't tell me.'

'I didn't want to tell you. We removed the spleen with a sizable mass and sent the biop to State. Could be lymphoma. And his kidney values are through the roof. We'll watch him a couple of days before he goes home.'

'Oh,' she said, tears coming. She loved Homer for reasons she didn't completely understand. 'How many mLs?'

'Eighty-six. And don't worry, Hal and Amanda will take good care of him.' Hal was subbing tomorrow and Tuesday, and Amanda would be watchful.

It would always be like this with Dooley's work. 'Tomorrow,' she said to Homer; she would come back tomorrow and hold him.

Across the aisle, a pup whined, urgent, thumping its tail.

Whose pup is this?' she said.

'Don't know yet.'

'A Golden puppy! What's the matter with him?'

'Her. Nothing. She's in perfect health.' He waited, gaining confidence. 'Amanda just gave her a good run.'

Lace squatted down, offered the back of her hand to the cold nose. 'I love her, she's adorable. Is someone boarding her?'

'That would be me.' Predicting doom, he took a deep breath. 'She's your wedding present.'

She looked up at him, and there was the light in her eyes and her great smile and the laughter—all the confirmation he needed to see—and she opened the crate and the pup barreled out and she got a good licking on her face, the whole deal, and she was happy, she was happy.

At that moment, he came into possession of a new and simple truth: if Lace was happy and Jack Tyler was happy, he was happy.

Lace sat on the floor; the pup rolled onto her back and offered her belly for a scratch.

'I love her!' said Lace. 'Jack Tyler will love her. You shouldn't have,' she said, making a joke.

'True,' he said.

She stood and gave him a hug. 'Thanks. She's beautiful. Now yours.'

Harley and Willie had hung it this morning on the big wall behind the reception desk. It would be the first time she had seen it hanging, but she wouldn't look yet; she would look when Dooley looked.

'Close your eyes.' She led him into the reception area. 'I'm closing mine, too.'

The pup sprawled on the cool tile of the floor, teething a treat.

With all her might, she hoped it was everything it needed to be—for Dooley and for all the people who would see it over the years—and for herself, too; she needed it to exceed her hard critique.

'Okay, we can look now.' Her heart beat in her temples. 'Your wedding present.'

Yes, yes, *yes*.

She heard the small exhale, the intake of his breath. He put his arm around her, shook his head with wonder. 'Man,' he said. 'Man.' It was all he could say.

On a canvas measuring three feet wide by two feet high, Dr. Kavanagh's farm truck zoomed by the viewer, hauling in the long bed five old dogs, including Barnabas. The doc himself was driving, you could tell by the splotch of cadmium red for his hair.

Kavanagh Animal Wellness Clinic, read the lettering on the passenger door. The very best Constable clouds she could possibly paint unfurled in a Carolina blue sky above the red truck. It was a beautiful day.

The Hershells had arrived early to give a hand where needed and would go home and come again for the ceremony.

'Mink and Honey Hershell, meet my brother, Henry Winchester, from Mississippi.'

As he reckoned, this was a lot to take in at a moment's notice. Henry was tall; he was short. Henry was handsome; he was plain. Henry was a Winchester; he was a Kavanagh. Henry was black; he was white—albeit with a farmer's tan.

Mink Hershell was speechless. But Honey was not.

'Lord help,' she said, 'y'all came all th' way from Mississippi? What kind of drivin' time is that?'

'Train time, Mrs. Hershell. I came up from Birmingham on th' Crescent. I'm very pleased to meet you.'

'Oh, my mother took th' Crescent from Philadelphia to New Orleans in 1979, th' only time she ever went out of state. She saved her ticket stub for ages. New Orleans was where my granddaddy died, he was a hundred and two. We're glad to have you, Mr. Winchester. I brought th' lima beans, I used a little side meat to season.'

'That's the way we like our limas back home,' said Henry.

'Which is your favorite? Green or white?'

'I like either one,' said Henry. 'But we usually eat them green for the higher manganese content.' Henry smiled. 'Good for the bones.'

'Well, great, I brought green. I'll remember that next time you come.'

'Henry,' said Mink, 'glad to have you. We sure think a lot of your brother here. He can grow grass like nobody's business.'

'What the guineas don't scratch up,' he said, grateful. He would remember Honey Hershell for this.

The luggage of his cousin Walter and Walter's wife Katherine had been sent to Colorado.

'Exactly what happened when we came for your wedding,' said Katherine, who was furious. 'I hate to be furious at a wedding, but what is the *matter* with those people? I *ask* you!'

He didn't know. He really didn't.

'I never have anything to *wear* down here, only lipstick and eye drops to my *name*.'

'What you're wearing is perfect,' said Cynthia.

'Jeans and a cotton sweater!' said Katherine. 'Nobody wears jeans to a southern wedding.'

'They do to this southern wedding. Trust me. And aren't those your good pearls you're wearing?'

'Yes, and thank God, or they'd be circling on a carousel in Denver.'

'Good pearls are all you ever need at a southern wedding,' said his wife. Such wisdom did not stick with Katherine Kavanagh of New Jersey.

'I am a recovering alcoholic for thirty years,' said Katherine. 'But how can I ever *fully* recover if I can't ever, even *once*, dress decently for a southern wedding?'

Walter drew him aside. 'Leave her alone a bit,' he said, 'she'll get over it. But I must say, what *is* the matter with those people?'

Nap time. She closed the door to the library and rocked him, slumped limp and solid against her heart, loving the bone and muscle of his body, his faint odor of grass and cookies and Golden Retriever.

Rocking, rocking, holding this wonderful sleeping boy, healing herself.

'How's the pup?' he asked Willie.

'Drinkin' water like crazy. Dooley set a bowlful on th' porch, an' when I looked a few minutes ago, it was empty. So I filled it an' she went after it again.'

Out of the blue, some inner voice, some awful premonition. Surely not . . .

'I could not watch th' door every minute,' said Lily.

'I understand,' he said, setting to work.

'In an' out, open an' shut, till you could lose your religion. I cannot believe anybody would bring a puppy home with all that's goin' on around here. Can you believe it?'

'Sort of,' he said, wiping the floor with paper towels. Slick.

'Who would think a puppy could stand up like a man and drag it off the table?'

'I'll need a mop,' he said.

'I'll get Arbutus to do it. Lord knows, we need walkie-talkies. You shouldn't be down on your knees like that, you're clergy.'

He laughed a little. But only a little.

The truck bed was filling up.

As hoped, the deviled egg was making a show for itself—three separate versions.

Green bean casserole—two dishes, same version: classic.

Fried chicken, none appearing to have come from KFC.

Coleslaw. Field peas. Baked ziti.

Twelve pounds of NC barbecue with a jug of sauce.

Four round cakes of cornbread to go with the barbecue, good thinking.

Five casseroles, covered, contents thereby defying iden-tification.

Honey Hershell's green limas and a supersize bowl of . . .

'Corn cut off th' cob, short-cooked with butter and a little sugar,' she told Willie. 'I don't feel like this should go in the bed of a truck. Mink will carry it to th' barn but you can take th' limas, they're in Tupperware and won't spill, an' please make sure I get my containers back.'

'Yes, ma'am,' said Willie.

At four-fifteen, the Hope House van pulled onto the north strip and dropped off four pans of biscuits shielded from the elements by Saran Wrap. 'Miss Louella's wedding present to Dr. Dooley and his bride,' said the driver, as proud as if he'd done the baking himself. 'If y'all could get th' pans back to us . . .'

Baked beans, warm from the oven. The inevitable potato salad, two containers full.

The even more inevitable store-bought rotisserie chicken in its plastic bag, but not to worry, as the Flower Girls would make it look good on the platter.

A salad fashioned with homegrown Boston lettuce and baby arugula in a wooden bowl.

'Don't let this get wilted,' said Judy the postmistress.

'No, ma'am,' said Willie.

'And don't let anybody else take this bowl home. My grandmother worked her bread dough in that bowl. My name, phone number, and PO box are on the bottom.'

'Yes, ma'am,' said Willie.

'It only leaves th' house for weddings and funerals,' she said, hammering her point.

Various jars of homemade pickles, two sent by Lew Boyd, who had won awards in this genre. Two quart mason jars of peaches, golden in their syrupy nectar.

A gigantic meatloaf, sliced, covered in foil, and attended by a Post-it note to whoever was running the kitchen: *Posi-*

tively has to be heated at 350° for twenty minutes to bring out the flavor!

A box of Oreos with a twelve-pack of Snickers in a Food Lion bag.

Lily handed off an oatmeal cookie as Harley blew into the kitchen. 'Don't eat it all in one place,' she said. 'Where you goin' at a trot?'

'To meet Miss Pringle on th' North Strip. She'll need somebody to walk 'er to th' tent. That's a pretty good haul.'

'Call and ask her to drive to the front of the house, then take her car and park it.'

'A good idea if I ever heard it. Lord help, I can't half think.' Harley looked dazed. 'Wait a minute. She's already on th' road and don't carry a cell phone.'

'Meet her on the North Strip like you planned, jump in, an' drive her to th' house, then *park th' car.*' For crap's sake. Plus he was wearin' enough cologne to knock you down.

She shook her head in disbelief. Things around here would probably be pretty much like this till she was old and gray.

Beth came into the room with two glasses of iced tea. 'Father Tim's cousin and his wife are here, their luggage is not. Your dad is shooting everything, even the signage. And the puppy ate part of a ham and is in her crate sleeping it off.'

'No! Father Tim worked so hard . . .'

'She got away from Dooley and Jack Tyler, but all is well, not to worry. It's glorious out there, beyond beautiful. Seventy-two degrees, a cloudless sky. Awesome! And your dad gave me sheet music for a song he loves and . . .'

Beth was glowing, ecstatic.

'And?'

'And there's a really huge surprise for you and Dooley— for everybody, really.'

She didn't know about another surprise. A litter of kittens had been dropped off in their driveway this morning; people did this to country vets.

'Four legs or two?'

'Um. Eight.'

'*Eight?*'

'Eight. End of clue.'

'Give me one more?'

'Can't do it. Okay. We've got to get your hair thing done. That dress is a knockout.'

'I love, love my dress,' said Lace. 'It just slithers on.'

'You are breathtaking in that scrap of silk. Perfect! Now sit down.'

'Are you scared?' said Lace.

'Duh. Of course I'm scared. I'm used to singing with scads of people in a university choir. I've never done solos, much less after an hour's rehearsal with a group called the Ham Biscuits.'

'You'll be awesome. You were wonderful in rehearsal, you could make a CD.'

Beth brushed Lace's long hair. 'Are you scared?'

'More sort of buzzing, like I'm plugged into something.'

'You are plugged into something. Love! You look fabulous, you're a stick, I'm so jealous.'

'We're practically the same size.'

'In certain places,' said Beth. 'So I'm just weaving your hair in kind of a loose braid. You have a gob of hair! Then we'll put it in an updo and work in your hairpiece and flowers.'

'Dooley's mom made my hairpiece from the lining of her wedding suit.'

'It will be perfect with the stephanotis. Turquoise and cream. My fave!'

'So my dress was Olivia's slip—something borrowed. In this box is my wonderful necklace—something blue. My shoes are something new. And you're my something old.'

'Gee, thanks,' said Beth.

A knock on the door.

'Who is it?' said Beth.

'Me, Jack Tyler!'

Beth started for the door, but she got up herself, and ran to open it, and there he was, this small person with the hazel eyes and long lashes, and a bashed-in toy. Jack Tyler looked scrubbed.

'Which side?' said Jack Tyler. 'Lily said ask you.'

'Which side what?'

'To part my hair.'

She was startled. How could she not know the answer to such a simple question? There would be hundreds, really thousands, of questions. If she was going to be a mom, she would have to think fast.

Maybe for the first time since he came, she was awake to the astonishing reality of Jack Tyler. This was no longer the bereft child staring into the pond or the image of the little guy they held fast in their hearts for two years and prayed for every day. This was now and this was real.

'Sit here in front of the mirror.'

She picked up her comb and breathed out.

'Look at you. So handsome! Your hair is already wet from the shower, so let's just start combing and see where your part is.'

Jack Tyler stared at the reflection that was sort-of-kind-of himself, wearing the new T-shirt that said *Dog's Best Friend*. What if he needed to go back to being the other boy again and couldn't?

'There! It parts on the left side.' She was oddly thrilled by this specific information. Beth applauded.

Jack Tyler looked at the face of the mom in the mirror and thought he'd never seen anyone so pretty, not even on TV. Then he stared for a long time at the other person he had started being.

'Man!' he said in a whisper.

He'd rarely seen Pauline in high spirits or looking what he would call happy. Like many believers, she was convinced she didn't deserve happiness, though he'd tried to persuade her otherwise. Today, however, he saw a spark. A spark can ignite.

'Somethin' good just happened, Father, can I tell you?'

'Come and sit.' He patted the place beside him on the glider, where he was taking a breather before going up to dress.

'Can I start at th' top?'

'The very best place to start!'

'I know I've thanked you before, Father, and I want to thank you again for raisin' Dooley and giving him everything I never could. You don't have to say anything, I just wanted to make sure I got that in before tellin' you that back in January, Buck an' I started watchin' pool competitions on TV. Plus we decided to read everything we could find on th' game Sammy loves. Seems like th' more we crammed in, th' more it all leaked out.'

'I'm with you there!' he said.

'But it made me remember something I'd completely forgot. Years ago, when I started drinkin' so bad, I shot a few games of pool down in Holding. I remember that it felt really natural; I even won a few games. It meant a lot to me to win something.'

She smiled, glad for a long-missing piece that fit somewhere in the puzzle.

'Anyway, when Buck and me study th' game, we pray that one day I'll be able to watch Sammy play in person.'

'Good. Yes.'

The sudden radiance of her smile . . .

'God just gave me a special time with Sammy. In th' library. I got to watch him play. An' we talked about famous people who loved pool. Like President George Washington. The father of our country.'

Bread and wine, bread and wine.

'I'm sure by now he knows I'm his mother, but for that speck of time in th' library, I was just someone who could talk a little pool. I'll never forget it.'

He was expecting her usual tears, but none came. Only the look of a woman who refused to indulge loss and was celebrating gain.

He would pray with Dooley before the ceremony; Cynthia and Olivia would go up to Lace and Beth and lift a petition there.

In the room they would vacate tonight, his deacon helped him vest. 'How do you feel?' she said.

'Like I overnighted a semi to South Florida.'

'You should have waked me.'

'Why would I do that?'

'So we could both lose sleep and feel rotten together.'

The amazing thing with his wife is that she was sincere about this notion.

'We both carry a handkerchief,' he said. 'Monogrammed. Value pack! And as you know, we both love poetry.' He was thrilled with this small cluster of similarities.

'More telling than blood, I'd say.' She circled him as if he were the statue of David, albeit draped, eyeing every detail. In a sentimental gesture, she was wearing her wedding suit, which still fit, albeit missing a scrap of lining.

'You are too handsome for words.'

'Try a word or two, anyway,' he said.

'Distinguished.'

'Keep going.'

'Gorgeous.'

'You can stop there,' he said. 'And same to you.'

'I'm not too sure about the processional of old dogs wearing bow ties.'

'They'll be fine.'

'What's going to make them *process*? I mean, they'll all just lie down in the grass.'

'Not my department,' he said.

She flicked an imagined dust mote from his sleeve.

'If you had to choose just one word for the way you feel in your heart on this day of days,' she said, 'what word would it be?'

This day of days was bumper cars, a merry-go-round, a Ferris wheel with every seat stuck on top, surveying the view.

'Giddy,' he said. 'A girlish sort of word, but it works.'

'Perfect,' she said.

'Perfect is your word?'

'No. Giddy is the perfect word for how I feel, too.' She draped the gold-trimmed stole around his neck, fussed with its alignment in front. 'Just think, sweetheart. We have another anniversary coming up in September. We can do a renewal of our vows.'

'You're kidding.' He couldn't take another marital union. Not anytime soon, anyway.

'A reenactment, then—I get stuck in the bathroom and you come find me and we race down the street and eat OMC!'

'Well, maybe,' he said, laughing.

He sat with Dooley in the room off the glider porch. 'Father, we thank you from the deep place of our souls for your unending grace and mercy in Dooley's life. Thank you for patience that you may reward it, thank you for brokenness that you may mend it, thank you for love that you may enlarge it above our most heartfelt expectations.

'Thank you for working wonders in their pathway to marriage and for this exciting time of parenthood. Now teach, guide, comfort, and inspire them—as believers in the one true God, as loving husband and wife, as wise parents, and as thoughtful stewards of this good land and its many creatures. May Meadowgate always be a place where your compassion is practiced and your love freely shared.

'Through Jesus Christ our Lord.'

'Amen,' they said together.

'The Lord be with you,' he said to his son.

'And also with you, Dad. Thanks for everything.'

He was standing on the glider porch, out of view of early guests being seated in the tent, and running early himself by ten or fifteen minutes.

He looked out to the tree line with its dense stand of hardwood. Though Miss Sadie's place at the wedding dinner would go to Henry, she was definitely here—in the triumphal success of a thrown-away boy who had worked hard to become Dooley Kavanagh, DVM. She was here in Dooley's laughter, in his loose gait as he walked across to the clinic, perhaps even in the thoughtful way he was entering into this marriage. Because she had believed in Dooley and provided for his education and future, she would always be here.

'Miss Sadie,' he whispered.

'Yes, Father?' He could hear her say it, clear as a bell.

'You're the best.'

'Pshaw!' she said.

He checked out the gift table. A four-slice toaster in a box tied with barn twine—that would be Willie, Lord bless him. And Miss Pringle's contribution, which he knew to be towels, always a good thing, and Puny's sheets and pillowcases, can't miss with that, and right here, the box wrapped in turquoise tissue paper by his wife, and containing what the young couple surely needed most—a check. He had not missed out on the heady excitement of wedding money, himself, even at the age of sixty-two. Miss Sadie had given them a check for a thousand dollars, discreetly folded and slipped into his hand at the parish hall reception. With it, as best he could recall, they had bought a toaster, towels, and sheets . . .

Ah, and there came the press corps, consisting of one— the intrepid Vanita Bentley, features editor of the *Mitford Muse*, wearing her signature owl-like spectacles and spike heels. Though he had never personally worn spike heels, he knew full well that they would betray the wearer in heavy turf. Bury a spike heel in turf, as many brides and guests had done in his time, and whoa.

She hobbled toward him, expectant. 'Hey, Father, it's me, Vanita! Runnin' late, it was th' log trucks. I haven't seen you in ages. Where have y'all been?'

'Living the simple life,' he said, grinning. He was fond of Vanita.

'Let me take your picture in that gorgeous thingumajig. What's it called?'

She was clicking away before he could get his face in order.

'This is a stole and this is a chasuble . . .'

'Oh, my gosh, how do you spell it?' She dug in her camera bag and pulled out a notepad.

'I wouldn't bother to mention it, really.'

'With that beautiful dove on the front an' th' gold trim? Are you sure?'

'Absolutely certain. It would be a snooze for your readers.'

'It's a double-ring ceremony, right? That's what they say in town.'

'It is.'

'I love double-ring ceremonies. The info I have is, her name is Lacey Harper Harper. Is that a typo?'

'Harper is her middle name and her surname.'

She scribbled this journalistic verity on her notepad.

'So where's th' bull everybody's talkin' about? I have ten minutes, max, before goin' to th' tent.'

'Follow the sign,' he said, pointing to *Cattle This Way*. He had forgotten to dot the *i*. 'And remember, no flash during the ceremony.'

'Got it, Father. Is there any poop I should know about? These are my good shoes.'

'There's always poop on a farm,' he said. 'Just watch where you step.'

'Chickens or what? Just so I know.'

'Chickens, guineas, deer, dogs, raccoons . . .' He could go on.

'Oh, golly,' she said, gathering up her skirt with one hand and adjusting the camera strap with the other.

Willie walked up to the porch, looking boiled from his shower and eyeing Vanita headed to the chill pen.

'She's tearin' up th' yard in them shoes,' said Willie.

'She's aerating the lawn,' he said. 'Be thankful.'

Beth stood behind her. 'Okay, close your eyes.'

She felt the string of beads slip around her neck and heard the nearly soundless snap of the clasp.

This was a dream. But she was going to live it as if it were real.

'Now look at yourself! I mean, please, you are so gorgeous. No, no. You don't cry at your own wedding. I did, of course, but for all the right reasons. Now listen to me. Be careful where you step, you never know if the poop control got it all.'

'Okay.' She laughed, stood up, felt the dress flowing over her skin, over the pain . . .

'Are you all right?'

'I just need to take my pill.'

'I'll get it, where is it?'

'On the Britannica shelf, to the right.'

Beth brought the pill, the water. Everyone had served her for weeks, she was grateful beyond words for their help and support and unending generosity. She could never repay such sacrifice.

'You have *got* to get a full-length mirror in this house,' said Beth. 'The hemline is perfect, the shoes are darling—I'm crazy about the wedge—and the hair is fabulous. You are the bride of the century, okay? So remember you're loved by everyone who knows you, and from all I can see, also by Jack Tyler, who hardly knows you at all.'

Jack Tyler had watched her stuff his church suit in a box of giveaways and smiled for the first time since he came. He would be in the living room looking for her to come down; she could hardly wait to see him.

As she walked to the door with Beth, she didn't remember being so tall—and light, as if she were ether. Maybe this is what she'd heard about and thought impossible, this sense of walking on air.

'You look beautiful in turquoise,' she told Beth. 'It's totally mean of you to outshine the bride.'

'Impossible!' said Beth. They had a hug. 'Wait for me, I'll be down in a flash. And don't go through the kitchen or you'll smell like ham. And remember to be your full five feet nine! No slumping.'

Lace laughed. 'Buy a mirror, stand up straight, watch where you step. Anything else?'

Beth gave her a fond look. 'Go out there and be as happy as a bird with a french fry.'

*The Celebration and
Blessing of the Marriage of*

~

LACEY HARPER HARPER

and

DOOLEY RUSSELL KAVANAGH

~

MEADOWGATE FARM

*Farmer, North Carolina
June 14*

Celebrant .... The Reverend Timothy Andrew Kavanagh

Parents of the Bride .... Dr. and Mrs. Walter Anderson Harper

Parents of the Groom .... The Reverend and Mrs. Timothy
    Andrew Kavanagh

Maid of Honor .... Elizabeth Anne Middleton

Best Men .... Sammy Barlowe, Pooh Leeper

Lay Readers .... The Reverend James Bradley
    Cortland, Cynthia Clary Kavanagh, Dr. Harold Emerson Owen

Ring Bearer .... Jack Tyler
    We are thrilled to be fostering to adopt Jack Tyler and
    thanking God for bringing him into our family. Thank you
    for your prayers!
    A cord of three strands is not quickly broken.
        ECCLESIASTES 4:12

Flower Girl .... Rebecca Jane Owen

Canine Processional .... Jessie Leeper, canine usher
    Buckwheat, Bowser, Bodacious, and Bonemeal

Musicians .... The Ham Biscuits
    Tommy Ferguson, vocals, harmonica, mandolin, banjo, guitar
    Buddy Ellison, bass, guitar
    Jake Thomas, fiddle
    Lonnie Grant, banjo
    Jesse O'Neill, guitar

*Please see insert for The Ministry of the Word,
prayers, and hymns*

～

Processional: Please stand and sing with us

"*Love Divine, All Loves Excelling*" .... Wesley/Prichard

Greeting and Opening Prayer

Declaration of Consent

Presentation of the Bride

The Ministry of the Word

The First Reading

Genesis 2:4–9, 15–22 .... Dr. Harold Emerson Owen

The Second Reading

Colossians 3:12–17 .... Cynthia Clary Kavanagh

Hymn

"*All Things Bright and Beautiful*" .... Elizabeth Anne Middleton

The Holy Gospel

John 15:9–12 .... The Reverend James Bradley Cortland

Homily .... The Reverend Timothy A. Kavanagh

The Marriage

Exchange of Vows and Rings

The Lord's Prayer

Our Father, who art in heaven, hallowed be your name. Your
kingdom come, your will be done, on earth as it is in heaven.
Give us this day our daily bread, and forgive us our trespasses,
as we forgive those who trespass against us. And lead us not into
temptation, but deliver us from evil. For yours is the kingdom, and
the power, and the glory, for ever and ever.

Amen.

The Prayers of the People

    Congregation responds: *Amen*

The Blessing of the Marriage

The Peace

    Congregation responds: *And also with you*

The Recessional

⌣

Following the ceremony, please join us in the barn for the wonderful dinner you provided. Dancing on the porch to the sound of the famous Ham Biscuits!

⌣

Remembering with love and gratitude:

SADIE ELEANOR BAXTER

RUSSELL ADAM JACKS

⌣

Two are better than one
Because they have a good return for their labor;
If either of them falls down,
One can help the other up.
But pity anyone who falls
And has no one to help them up.
Also, if two lie down together, they will keep warm.
But how can one keep warm alone?

                           ECCLESIASTES 4:9–11

Thirteen

Wedding guests in general could be pretty clamor-
ous before a ceremony. But he found things unex-
pectedly serene beneath the tent, restful in a way.
A certain peace lay over the fields, over the people, over his
own heart.

He looked at his son. Dooley nodded; breathed in,
breathed out.

They stepped into the tent, into the welcome of music.

Not once in his priesthood had he heard the glad notes of
"Love Divine, All Loves Excelling" rendered by harmonica.
In the warmth of the June afternoon, he felt a chill down his
right leg as he processed the grassy aisle with the groom at
his side.

Joy of heaven, to earth come down,
Fix in us thy humble dwelling,

All thy faithful mercies crown.
Jesus, Thou art all compassion,
Pure unbounded love thou art . . .

Sammy and Pooh followed as the standing congregation gave forth its mighty best. There was Hal Owen's splendid baritone, Beth's crystal soprano . . .

Visit us with thy salvation,
Enter every trembling heart.

At the simple lectern made by Harley, he and Dooley embraced. The two best men peeled off to stand on Dooley's left.

Come, Almighty to deliver,
Let us all thy life receive . . .

And there was Jessie with the dogs sporting bow ties and coupled together by ribbons, a photo op of the first rank. Mid-hymn, phones and cameras were dug from pockets and handbags and there began the gleeful preoccupation that wedding guests so relish nowadays. Bowser swaggered, Bodacious looked doleful, Buckwheat effected a jaunt in his step. At row four, Bonemeal paused to sniff the shoes of Judy, the postmistress. Roughly on cue, the whole lot veered to the groom's side.

Clockwork, he thought.

Then Beth, in a turquoise frock and as radiant as any bride, came singing, heads turning . . .

Finish then thy new creation,
Pure and spotless let us be.

Let us see thy great salvation,
Perfectly restored in thee . . .

Now Rebecca Jane Owen and the strewing of the petals of Seven Sisters; carmine showering upon emerald grass . . .

As Lace and her father entered the tent with Jack Tyler, Dooley's left leg began to jiggle. He was aware of this, but his brain refused to send a nerve signal to stop it. He put his weight on his left leg, dug the heel of his loafer into the turf, and locked his knee.

He had occasionally perceived marriage to be a cosmic black hole, void of anything at all. At the sight of Lace, the science of his heart perceived the void filled with galaxies beyond number.

Lace walked the aisle on the arm of Doc Harper, the afternoon light dancing gold over her dress. She was taking the day not by force, as he could plainly see, but by grace, and smiling at him as if to say, Hooray, we have come through.

In the hand placed upon her father's arm, she held the bouquet. In the other, she held Roo, pressed to her heart. At her side, Jack Tyler, in his plaid pants, carried the pillow. Cautious and solemn he came, as if walking on eggs.

Necks craned to get a better look at the bride and the little boy mentioned in the program, who was such a surprise to all, such a hope, really. An electrical current made a buzz through the congregation.

Changed from glory into glory,
Till in heaven we take our place . . .

All this. All this coming to him, entering into him, Dooley Kavanagh. For a split second, he blanked, then came to. He steadied himself, thinking his heart could actually, though not probably, explode and he would be toast right here in front of everybody. But he was ready. He was completely ready for the tide that had the power to lift him off his feet and sweep him away.

Till we cast our crowns before Thee,

Lost in wonder, love, and praise.

The music ended, the congregation was seated. Lace looked down to Jack Tyler and gave him a smile and a nod and he walked to Beth and stood by her side near the seated musicians.

'Who gives this woman to be married?'

'Her mother and I,' said Hoppy. He kissed the cheek of his daughter and stepped to the front row and sat by Olivia and strapped on his Nikon.

To Dooley on his left and to Lace on his right, he, Timothy, celebrant and father, extended his hands to the couple and drew them as one to face him.

'Dearly beloved: We have come together in the presence of God to witness and bless the joining together of this man and this woman in Holy Matrimony.

'The bond and covenant of marriage was established by God in creation, and our Lord Jesus Christ adorned this manner of life by his presence and first miracle at a wedding in Cana of Galilee . . .'

He was twain, speaking by heart the words he had learned

so long ago, and at the same time conscious of the assembly beneath the shade of the tent.

To his left on the groom's side, his wife and Henry and Walter and Katherine, kith and kin, his own heart's blood, and . . . good Lord! Kenny! With his wife, Julie, and two small children. How had he not known this?

He gulped air, and joy with it. Dooley and his brothers had seen them, too.

'The union of husband and wife in heart, body, and mind is intended by God for their mutual joy, for the help and comfort given one another in prosperity and adversity. Therefore marriage is not to be entered into unadvisedly or lightly, but reverently, deliberately, and in accordance with the purposes for which it was instituted by God.

'Into this holy union Lace Harper and Dooley Kavanagh now come to be joined.'

'Kenny,' Dooley whispered.

He got the cue. 'Will you, Kenneth Barlowe, come forward and stand with us as a best man to your brother?'

Every eye was on Kenny Barlowe, who didn't especially resemble the brothers standing behind the priest. This one was of heavier build, with dark brown hair. That's the way it is with cattle, thought Mink Hershell. Sometimes you put two Red Angus together and get the Wild coloration, which is basically spotted.

Kenny kissed Lace on the cheek, hugged his brothers. In the congregation, a couple of handkerchiefs fluttered out.

'I require and charge you, Dooley and Lace, here in the

presence of God, that if either of you know any reason why you may not be lawfully united in marriage, and in accordance with God's word, you do now confess it.'

A June breeze carried the breath of roses to those assembled. It seemed to Olivia Harper that time stood still. She held the hand of her husband, who had granted her a new heart in more ways than one.

'Lace, do you take Dooley to be your husband; to live together in the covenant of marriage? Do you vow to love him, cherish him, honor and keep him, in sickness and in health, and forsaking all others, be faithful to him until death do you part?'

'I do.'

'Dooley, do you take Lace to be your wife; to live together in the covenant of marriage? Do you vow to love her, cherish her, honor and keep her, in sickness and in health, and forsaking all others, be faithful to her until death do you part?'

'I do.'

'Do those of you witnessing these promises vow to do all in your power to uphold Lace and Dooley in their marriage?'

'We do!'

The farm dogs slept, studied the crowd, yawned. Bowser licked himself with some vigor until Jessie gave him a shove with her foot.

'The Lord be with you!' he said to all assembled.

'And also with you!'

Danny Hershell had not been at his mama and daddy's

wedding for th' reason that he wasn't born yet, but at one wedding he'd been at, they had lots of balloons and th' bride had rode in on a mule an' at th' end her an' her husband had rode off on a tractor. But this deal right here was one of the most different kind of thing he'd ever seen.

'Let us pray. O gracious and ever living God, you have created us male and female in your image. Look mercifully upon Dooley and Lace, who come to you seeking your blessing, and assist them with your grace, that with true fidelity and steadfast love they may honor and keep the promises and vows they make, through Jesus Christ our Savior, who lives and reigns with you in the unity of the Holy Spirit, one God, forever and ever. Amen.'

'Amen!'

Love, cherish, honor, keep. A handful! Honey Hershell hoped these kids had thought it over carefully, but even if they had, they would still not have a clue. You never had a clue about anything till it happened and you learned the truth about yourself.

Vanita Bentley fiddled with her camera to adjust the setting for shade. *In sickness and in health* was the kicker. If it wadn't for her income from the *Muse* and the check from the government, she an' Donny Bentley would be livin' in a tent on the creek. First a broken leg on his job with NCDOT, then an infection, then the gangrene which they couldn't hardly control and now the crutch and all the doctor appointments and here were these kids opting for the same thing if push ever came to shove. She would put them on the prayer list at

First Baptist and if th' church secretary said why do they need prayer, they just got married, she would say, Please! That is th' whole point.

Mink Hershell reckoned he had slept through a bunch of Scripture reading and maybe even somebody singing, which he sort of felt guilty about except he'd been up half the night checking out th' wind damage and had to put oil in the tractor before taking it over to what he still called the Owen place but was now the Kavanagh place. He guessed he hadn't snored or Honey would have given him a jab. With the Baptists, of which he was one, it didn't take forever and a day to get married. This crowd was plowin' through the whole Bible before they would let a man kiss his wife. He consulted his program. Looks like he'd slept through the reading from Genesis and woke up in the Gospel of John.

'This is my commandment,' Father Brad read aloud, 'that you love one another as I have loved you. The Word of the Lord.'

'Thanks be to God!' said the people.

Mink leaned toward his wife. 'What's a homily?'

'Lace, you recently asked two very thoughtful questions. Is cherish the same as love? And how do we cherish someone?

'I believe cherish to be a higher plane within the context of love, something like the upstairs level in a home. Love must come first, for without it, it would be impossible to access the higher and perhaps even nobler realm of cherishing and holding dear.

'So how can we cherish another? Might there be one powerful but simple method that leads to the richness we find in the act of cherishing the beloved?

'As I studied and prayed, there it was. In Romans 12:10. A one-word marriage manual in a vigorous, no-nonsense verb.

'Outdo.

'"Outdo one another," says Paul, "in showing honor."

'What outdo means, of course, is going above and beyond. Outdo means pressed down, shaken, and running over.

'What outdo does not mean is a competition in which one person wins the game and the other loses. To outdo one another means you both win. In Ephesians 5:28, we're told that he who loves his wife loves himself. In effect, a good marriage happens when the happiness of the other is essential to your own happiness. We might say that a good marriage is a contest of generosities.

'How wonderful that it's possible to ensure our own happiness by seeking the happiness of another. Is it our job to make the beloved happy? It is not. The other person always has a choice. It is our job to generously outdo, no matter what, and discover that the prize in this contest of generosity is more love.

'All of which moves two outdoers in a circle, like the rings that will be exchanged today. Dooley cherishes Lace, Lace cherishes Dooley, and the circle is unbroken. It is definitely a practice of love that requires the participation of two. If only one is outdoing, that one will soon be done in.

'So we love and that is good. We cherish and that is even better.

'I would ask you to remember that you're not only husband and wife, you are also brother and sister in Christ and mother and father to Jack Tyler. Here are three opportunities to outdo without being done in, to refresh and fulfill yourselves as others outdo themselves for you.

'I believe many of us simply *do*. And sometimes that seems a gracious plenty. But in *out*doing, if each is giving and receiving, there's always something circling back, helping to replenish our emotional and physical strength as we help replenish theirs.

'I'll close with a very specific way to help you live the principle of outdoing. This is a key to opening hearts, a gentle pathway to cherishing your beloved. To that end, I have been given this further word.

'Listen.

'Listening is among the most generous ways to give. When a loved one talks to us—whether their words appear to be deep or shallow—listen. For in some way, they are baring their souls.

'Listen, dear Lace. Listen, my son. And you will cherish and be cherished.

'In the name of the Father and of the Son and of the Holy Spirit. Amen.'

'Amen!'

There was a pause; the congregation consulted their programs. This was the official Marriage part, the big one.

Dooley caught his breath and recited after his dad. 'In the name of God, I, Dooley, take you, Lace, to be my wife, to have and to hold from this day forward, for better, for worse, for richer, for poorer, in sickness and in health . . .'

He felt the thud of his heart literally stopping its beat.

Choo-Choo was standing just beyond the entrance to the tent, looking in. Behind him, three heifers cropped grass. His heart seemed now to fill his throat. If he asked everyone to remain seated and the bull came plowing into their midst . . . if he asked them to leave the area quietly and the cattle grew alarmed . . . there were no rubrics for this.

'Choo-Choo,' he whispered to Dooley and Lace.

They turned around. Lace moved at once to Jack Tyler and took his hand.

'Ladies and gentlemen, I caution you to sit very still. Please do not turn around at this time or make any sudden movement.'

Harley turned around at once. 'God A'mighty!'

Now everybody turned around. Gasps. A yelp here and there, followed by a terrified silence in which Jack Tyler began to cry.

The musicians rose from their chairs in slow motion, instruments in hand. 'We've got your back,' Tommy said to Dooley.

Dooley spoke without taking his eyes off the bull. 'Th' chill gate's too close to th' tent to try and run 'em in there. Open th' cattle gate, Dad.'

'The keys,' he said, faint with alarm.

'In th' truck. Drive it like you stole it.'

'Look out for Cynthia,' he said.

He moved like a snowball melting, vanished behind the woodshed, jumped in the truck, heard the astonishing sound of music: 'When the Saints Go Marching In.'

He didn't look back.

It took maybe sixty seconds to drive to the cattle gate, but it seemed an eternity.

Choo-Choo was plenty smart, but not that smart.

Somebody had left the gate open.

On his way back, he saw them coming and stopped the truck and turned off the ignition. Tommy and his band were walking backward, playing music. The cattle followed, curious and definitely interested.

Dooley kept to their rear; slow motion, everything in slow motion.

Lord, I want to be in that number when the saints . . .

They were headed toward the open gate.

'Easy,' Dooley was saying. 'Easy, now.'

The wedding party was scattered around the lawn, under the tent, out by the woodshed.

Doc Owen's voice, a bullhorn of its own: 'Thirty-minute break, everybody, and back here to finish the job! Six o'clock sharp!'

Most headed to the house; Danny and his brother, Rudy, disappeared into the bushes.

As for the guy in white vestments, he had broken a cold sweat; he was trembling.

'Jesus,' he said as his wife came running, looking relieved.

In the kitchen, Dooley was drinking water, Jack Tyler was drinking water, everybody was drinking water while the pup looked out from her crate with an accusing eye.

High fives with the band.

'You boys ever tried to make it in Nashville?' Doc Owen asked the banjo player, Lonnie Grant.

'Been there, done that, got th' T-shirt,' said Lonnie. 'Not doin' that again.'

The kitchen hadn't expected this invasion. They were trying to get dinner to the barn, for Pete's sake; Lily could hardly move from the stove to the back door. But everybody was happy now and Jack Tyler had got over his crying spell and that was good enough for her—she liked happy people.

'So, Dad.'

Dooley took him aside, said something that couldn't be printed in a family newspaper. 'It was me.'

'What was you?'

'I left the cattle gate open.'

What could he say? 'It's okay. You're allowed one today.' He managed a small laugh. 'But only one!'

Mink Hershell checked his watch. The tent was filling up again—great, but the break was longer than thirty minutes.

Seven days a week, Honey had supper on the table at five-thirty sharp except when they drove to Mitford to the Feel Good. He looked at his program. Lord knows, he didn't re-member this much hoo-ha when he married Honey twenty— or was it nineteen?—years ago. He had picked her up at her mama's house and they had arrived together at the church in his daddy's hearse. He remembered that the preacher thought it was a limo.

Deviled eggs. He hoped they would have deviled eggs. And ham! What would a wedding be without deviled eggs and ham? As for diggin' up th' bourbon, yes, he would go with th' diggers, but he would not touch a drop, he would just watch.

Everybody was back in the tent now and there came Father Tim with his robe thing flyin', and the wedding party—all but the dogs—trailing behind and cracking up, and the musicians at the end. All assembled gave the musicians a hand. 'Woohoo, Biscuits!' 'Go, Biscuits!' Like that.

The newspaperwoman scooted into the chair next to him and Honey. Boy howdy, this deal would give her somethin' to write about.

He gathered with the wedding party at the homemade lectern as before. Yet nothing really seemed as before—they were live-wired, jets burning in some new and wondrous way.

With no warning whatsoever, just boom, there came the celebrant's tears.

'Hey, Dad,' whispered Dooley. 'You're cryin' at my wedding.'

'As promised,' he said, realizing he had no handkerchief.

Lace handed over a small linen square that had belonged to Miss Sadie, and she and Dooley had a good laugh. He took it and wiped his eyes and there came his own laughter—more laughter than he'd had in a good while—and then everybody was laughing; it had gone viral.

Mink timed how long it took people to finish laughing. It was lasting a long dern time, maybe because they had a lot of stress to let out after lookin' a bull in the eye. Or maybe it was something like he'd read about—people laughing in church because of the Holy Spirit gettin' loose. Oh, *Lord*, when would these people ring th' dinner bell and get on with it?

'In the name of God, I, Dooley, take you, Lace, to be my wife, to have and to hold from this day forward, for better, for worse, for richer, for poorer, in sickness and in health, to love and to cherish, come rain or come shine. This is my solemn vow.'

'In the name of God, I, Lace, take you, Dooley, to be my husband, to have and to hold from this day forward, for better, for worse, for richer, for poorer, in sickness and in health, to love and to cherish, come rain or come shine. This is my solemn vow.'

'In the name of the Father, the Son, and the Holy Spirit, I pronounce you husband and wife.'

Beth led Jack Tyler forward with the pillow. He was really tired of holding this stupid pillow and would do anything to quit. It was like a shade started coming down over his head, over his eyes, he could not wait to either lie down in the grass or eat a Snickers bar, which he'd seen come out of a grocery bag in the kitchen.

The dad's brother named Kenny took one of the rings and gave it to Granpa Tim, who gave it to the dad.

'Bless, O Lord, these rings to be signs of the vows by which this man and this woman have bound themselves to each other, through Jesus Christ our Lord.'

If his leg started jiggling . . . 'Lace, I give you this ring as a symbol of my vow and with all that I am, and all that I have, I honor you . . . in the name of the Father, and of the Son, and of the Holy Spirit.'

She felt it slipping onto her finger, felt the steadiness of Dooley's hand as he placed it there. A simple gold band, just what she wanted; it was a kind of nourishment.

Jack Tyler watched Uncle Sammy take the other ring off the pillow and hand it to Granpa Tim, who handed it to the mom.

'Dooley, I give you this ring as a symbol of my vow, and with all that I am, and all that I have . . .' She caught her breath. 'I honor you, in the name of the Father, and of the Son, and of the Holy Spirit.'

He felt the warmth of her touch as she slipped it on his finger. He was plastic in a microwave.

Beth took the pillow from Jack Tyler, who stretched out his arms for Roo. Nobody else had ever touched Roo except his granny, who sometimes would hide Roo for days. He smelled Roo to see if he smelled different.

Then Uncle Pooh reached in his pocket and pulled something out and gave it to the granpa and the granpa gave it to the mom. He laid Roo in the grass and held hands with the mom and the dad and they stood in front of the granpa.

He'd said it over and over in his mind, and the mom and the dad said they would squeeze his hand at the right time to say it out loud. 'Say it in your very biggest voice,' the mom had told him.

'Dooley, Lace, and Jack Tyler . . . we honor you today as a family.'

'Amen!' said the people.

'Forever.'

'Amen!'

'For better or for worse. To love and to cherish.'

'Amen!'

The hand squeeze. 'Come rain or come shine!' yelled Jack Tyler, and all the people laughed and clapped.

The mom leaned down and took his left hand and put a ring on his finger and looked in his eyes really close. 'We're a family now, Jack Tyler.' She kissed him on one side of his face. 'This is forever.'

His dad squatted down and kissed him on the other side of his face and looked in his eyes and said, 'We're a family now, Jack Tyler. We'll be a family forever.'

'Those whom God has joined together let no one put asunder!' said the granpa in a really loud voice.

He grabbed Roo, his dad picked him up and the people clapped and clapped and somebody whistled and the bass fiddle went *whoom, whoom, whoom,* and not knowing exactly what else to do, he held Roo up high so everybody could see his best friend.

Second row back on the groom's side, Henry removed his handkerchief and pressed it to his eyes. He wished his mother could see this, but he would tell her everything, everything. Since coming up from Charlotte this morning, he was surprised to realize that he no longer thought about Eva every day. In one way or another, she had occupied his thoughts for nearly forty years. A bird sang—Eva. A stylish woman boarded the train—Eva. Hearing a church choir—Eva, whose voice was honey distilled from clover.

The dark-skinned girl in the black hat with the red rose had swept him off his feet in the truest sense; he remembered the strange weakness in his ankles as she boarded his train the first time, as if the bones had become the brittle bones of a bird.

Eva was dying of a rare type of brain cancer and he should have insisted, or somehow wrangled a marriage license without her consent, for he wanted with all his being to be legally bound to the crucifying pain and to her death for as long as it took. But her mother had passed and Eva had disappeared. The cruelest hurt he had ever known or would know. Just gone. A lifetime of loving had been compressed into eleven months that he would remember for the rest of his days.

He looked with tenderness at the young couple who had overcome so much of their own loss and sorrow and in the bloom of their youth were given this fine little boy, a gift from God.

Indeed, it was God who had urged him to make this trip into the eastern highlands, tracing his bloodline to his brother. And he was satisfied. Seeing the young family finding their way together was a benediction—something in him felt healed and healing.

Tommy grinned. He'd never heard so many amens, and he'd been raised Baptist. A lot of stuff had made his hair stand up today—Choo-Choo breathing down their necks, for one. But he was no hero, he'd been scared out of his mind to walk the guys toward the cattle and then lead a bull and three heifers all the way to the gate. Bulls could be plenty mean, even kill people, and a heifer could get her back up, too. How did he know the music would work? He'd seen something on YouTube where a few French dudes got together and played music and the cows loved it. But it was totally rolling the dice, what they'd done today, and with way too much at stake. After they got the cattle back in the field, his legs had turned to mush.

And Beth—she made his hair stand up, for sure. Run a wet finger around a fragile glass with water in it and out comes the shining, haunting sound in her voice, something pure as spring water on his granddaddy's place, or maybe sheer as silk but strong as a tow sack. He put his hand on the neck of his old archtop and felt the reassurance of it. He'd brought his favorite axe for this and would flat-pick for the recessional and the dancing.

She stood so close he could touch her. He smiled along her back and the curve of her shoulders, and wondered if that was her perfume or was it the roses. He probably wouldn't tell her that her voice reminded him of a tow sack. So what would he tell her before she left tonight? That was the question.

'Wake up!' Honey said to her husband. 'It's th' Prayers of th' People.'

'Eternal God!'

Doc Owen's baritone boomed out a prayer. 'Amen!' said the people.

Jack Tyler laid his head on the dad's shoulder and slept. Roo fell into the grass.

The program quivered lightly in Pauline Leeper's hands. She would not weep as she was wont to do in anything associated with her children. She could at least do that for them.

'Give us grace when we hurt each other . . . to recognize and acknowledge our fault, and to seek each other's forgiveness and yours.'

'Amen!'

She realized she had said the prayer incorrectly. It read, Give *them* grace when *they* hurt each other . . . and acknowledge *their* fault. She had deeply humiliated herself.

Buck Leeper did not notice his wife's revision of the prayer. He squeezed her hand as she sat down, knowing that he couldn't have made it without her. She hadn't saved his life, exactly, nor he hers. Two hopeless drunks had pushed and pulled together, mostly fifty-fifty, and by the grace of God, they had each made themselves a gift offering to the other. He knew it couldn't have happened if he hadn't prayed with Father Tim that night in the rectory. *Thank you, God, for loving me and for sending your Son to die for my sins. I sincerely repent of my sins and receive Christ as my personal savior. Now as your child, I turn my entire life over to you.* So simple. So mighty.

There would be healing with her children, he could feel it. His heart swelled with some new hope as he read his part in the Prayers of the People.

Harley cleared his throat and stood. He would rather take a whipping.

'Make their life together a sign of Christ's love to this sinful and broken world . . .' He paused briefly and carried on. '. . . that unity may overcome . . .' He did not like this next word, it was long as a coal train . . . '*estrangement*, forgiveness heal guilt, an' joy conquer despair.' Breathing like a man reprieved, he sat. How anybody could make heads or tails out of that he didn't know.

'Amen!'

Mink Hershell squirmed in his chair. The torment of it. Sure, he thought the world of Dooley and Lace and the little kid was a blessing, but it looked like they'd be in this tent till the cows came home, which they already *did*, in case nobody noticed.

'Stay awake,' said Honey.

He was cured of weddings; he'd rather go to a funeral.

Third row back on the bride's side, Agnes Merton, longtime sexton of Holy Trinity Church up the holler, was signing the ceremony for her son, Clarence, deaf since early childhood. The signing came so naturally to her that she was able also to dwell, however briefly, on her affection for the celebrant.

Father Tim's stability had been a spiritual banquet, nay, a lifesaver, for her and for Clarence. All those years she and her son had worked in the forsaken little church, so remote from anyone, and then he had come, this good man—fording the creek, climbing the mountain, and ending up in their lives, a sweet savor of the one true Father. Oh, he was fully human—could even be a mite snappish at times, but that was the worst of it.

Father Tim lifted his arms. 'God the Father, God the Son, God the Holy Spirit, bless, preserve, and keep you: the Lord mercifully with his favor look upon you, and fill you with all spiritual benediction and grace; that you may faithfully live together in this life, and in the age to come have life everlasting.'

'Amen!'

'The peace of the Lord be always with you!'

'And also with you!'

Danny Hershell had read the program and knew this was it, it was now or never.

'Kiss th' bride!' he hollered. What was wrong with people in this religion that guys didn't get to kiss th' bride? His mama would kill him, but she had killed him before any number of times.

The crowd applauded big-time. And ol' Dooley, he leaned over and laid one on her. Then he, Danny Do-Right Hershell, did what had to be done, though nobody had asked him to do it: he rang the cowbell loud as he could.

Everybody was standing, people clapping, cheering, Doc Harper running up th' aisle with his camera, and whoa—the musicians playin' somethin' really cool and for sure not out of a church songbook an' there came th' bride and Dooley and th' little guy still asleep.

Honey gave Mink a look. 'You half kill 'im,' she said, 'an' I'll handle th' other half.'

Say la vee, they had a boy who was out of control, a factor that came from her side, which was Irish. He sighed deeply and took Honey's pocketbook off the knob of her chair and slung it over his shoulder. He carried it for her everywhere but never asked anymore what was in it. Blow-dryer, a Bible-study book that weighed more than a refrigerator, a quart jar of beans to give a neighbor, her entire makeup kit with twenty shades of eye shadow, Lord knows.

The music was crankin', two or three people were dancin' in the aisle, he was out of here.

Fourteen

While Jack Tyler was in the hall room they ducked across to the library and collapsed on the sofa, and there came Doc Harper with his Nikon.

'Okay, hold it,' said the bride's dad, backing up to the pool table.

'There you go.' Flash, flash. 'Beautiful.' Flash, flash. 'Okay, smile at the camera, perfect.' Flash. 'Now kiss the bride, we got some great shots in the tent.' Flash, flash. 'Laughing is good, fine, wonderful.' Flash, flash, flash.

'And here comes our boy!' said the photographer, stepping out to the hallway. 'Hold it, buddy. Right there. Give me a smile, there you go, like th' pants. Okay, walk this way, keep coming, good, great, we're done—posterity is served. You'll thank me for this, guys. See you at the barn.'

'You can quit your day job, Doc!'

She loved seeing her parents so happy. At some weddings, only one side of the aisle was happy.

'I'm hungry,' said Jack Tyler.

'We are, too,' she said. 'But we're going to look at our rings first.'

'Why?'

'Because there's a surprise inside.'

'What?'

'Take yours off and we'll see.'

Dooley turned on the lamp by the sofa and helped Jack Tyler remove the small band—it was a bit of a tug.

He held the ring under the light and squinted at the inscription. 'See that really tiny word? It says . . . forever.'

Jack Tyler took a deep breath.

'That's how long we're going to be a family,' said Dooley.

'How long is forever?' His old granny said his real dad was gone forever and his real mom went gone forever next.

Lace slipped his ring on again, the ring she had bought based strictly on hope. 'Forever is always.'

'I won't go back to my old granny ever?'

'You will be with us and we will be with you. Forever.'

He stood close to the mom and put his hand on her knee. Her shining dress was soft and smooth, and she leaned over and kissed the top of his head.

'Is there words in your ring?'

She didn't know. She hoped; she really, really hoped. But maybe not.

'Read your ring,' said her husband.

Yes! He had done it! She was happy in a small way she hadn't known before.

Jack Tyler crowded so close he could feel the mom's breath on his face. Something was going off in him like firecrackers because of the magic stuff that was happening with rings.

She leaned to her husband and kissed him on the cheek. 'Love you always!'

She removed her ring and in the light of the lamp read the minuscule words inside the band.

Love you always back.

'You're crying at your own wedding,' he said.

So much happiness. It seemed dangerous, reckless.

Jack Tyler slumped to the floor. 'I'm *hungry*.'

'One more to go, buddy.' Dooley removed his gold band, peered at the engraving.

Cherish.

He gave her a long look. 'We can definitely do that,' he said.

Heading to the barn, Julie carried the giant meatloaf and Cynthia the loaves of bread packed into a box.

'We're so happy you could come, Julie. It's the cream in the jug, as the Brits like to say.'

'My family adores Kenny and we're very close to his grandparents. There are lots of us in Oregon, but he misses his brothers and sister. Right now his work is seriously demanding, and with the house payments . . . but we prayed about finding a way to come and then the tickets showed up. We knew we were meant to be here.'

'It's a whodunit!'

'No note, nothing to say who the sender was. And business class! We were thrilled. Lace thought it might have been her parents, but they deny it.' Julie gave her a smile. 'Did you and Father Tim do it?'

'I'd love to take credit for such generosity, but no, we were convinced you couldn't come because of work.'

'We didn't call to say we were coming, we just thought, Here are the tickets, of course we're going. It was so interesting that no one seemed to expect us.'

She liked this pretty young woman who was twenty-four but looked like a schoolgirl and who, at five foot three, was a perfect bookend to herself.

They handed off their provender to Lily, who passed it along to Arbutus, who, in tandem with Violet, made the distributions.

'If you could sit with Etta while I put Ethan to bed after dinner, I'd really appreciate it.'

'I'd like nothing better.'

People were gathering at the shed, and a group tour was headed their way from the chicken lot.

'Everyone seems to enjoy visiting the chickens,' said Julie.

'Wait till they bring in the llamas!' She was excited about the possibility; there would definitely be a book in it. Maybe a pop-up this time.

It had come to her just now, the urgency. She must feed on God's grace and she must hurry. If she waited beyond this day, she might never see her sons again—Sammy was leaving tomorrow; Kenny and his family would be gone early Tuesday. The words she read aloud in the ceremony had spoken directly to her. '. . . to recognize and acknowledge our fault and seek each other's forgiveness.'

She could not ask their forgiveness. That was asking too much. She had long recognized her sin toward her children, and now her job was to acknowledge it through one simple admission. She had declined to give such admission all these years; instead, she and Pooh and Jessie and Dooley had stepped over and around what some called the elephant in the room.

This simple admission was all that God wanted of her right now, she felt certain of it. To forgive or not to forgive would be their choice.

He was searching for a backup cake server for the barn when Pauline came into the kitchen, out of breath. She had been looking for him, she said.

'I need to tell my children I'm sorry.'

'Yes.'

'Sammy will be leaving and Kenny . . .'

'I understand.'

'Pray for me, please. Pray that I won't cry. I don't want to do that to them.'

He nodded yes, crossed himself.

She looked desperate. 'Is there anything you can tell me, Father?'

'God is with you. Speak the name Jesus if you can't do more. He's listening.'

She tried to breathe.

'I just saw Sammy in the library,' he said. 'He'll be coming down to the barn in a few minutes. And Kenny is getting something out of their rental car at the front door.'

Both of them at once . . . if she could hold back the tears, she could do anything.

She would no longer use the crutch of blaming their father or the old, disastrous craving over which she tried to believe she had no control—blaming, always blaming someone or something—and she would no longer try to believe that her dues had been paid in that terrible fire years ago.

She stepped out to the porch. This was the hardest. Of all her heedless acts of disgrace, giving her son into the hands of a stranger had been the most unforgivable.

He closed the hatch of the car and looked up. He was holding a diaper and a sippy cup.

'I'm sorry,' she said. She couldn't speak above a whisper.

Kenny felt his heart cracking open like a geode. Someone

had sent the tickets anonymously; they just showed up in the mail. He'd known that if they came to the wedding, it would come to this.

To forgive her was the right thing. It's what God asks people to do and what Julie would want him to do. He actually felt a certain compassion for this woman who he didn't know. To forgive her would free him in ways he couldn't imagine, maybe even to be a better husband and father. But he could not.

'For everything,' she whispered.

'I'm sorry, too,' he said. 'Sorry I can't forgive you for handing me off to a stranger. Sorry you're not even anybody I remember.'

She watched him walk around the corner of the house, toward the barn and his life in Oregon and the years of his future. She had added to his sorrow, not subtracted. She could not seem to stop hurting the people she loved.

Sammy stood by the table with a cue, squinting at the balls on the felt.

She forced herself to walk into the library, felt her chest heave with the pounding of her heart.

Sammy concentrated on the table, not looking up. The set of his jaw, an old scar livid on his cheek; he knew who had come into the room.

'I'm sorry,' she said. 'So sorry.'

'No,' he said. He stood like a statue, refusing to look at her. 'No.'

She would not force anything from him, nothing at all. She turned and walked away on legs that would barely support her and went into the hall room and locked the door and lifted the seat.

'Jesus,' she said, weeping, and vomited into the toilet.

Dooley. Her spoken repentance could be a gift to him or it could be a stone. She prayed against the stone. If she waited beyond this day, she would be free to keep believing the old lie that Dooley understood, that it was all forgotten, and she should forget it, too.

She thought maybe he had forgiven her, but there was no way of knowing. Throughout his school days in Virginia and Georgia and North Carolina, he often came to visit Pooh and Jessie. He was always open and kind with Buck, but distant from her. She hadn't known how to find again the small bond they had when he was little, before he went to her poor daddy and then to Father Tim. He had been the one she dumped the care of all the others on, and he'd done his very best and she had never even thanked him. No, they didn't talk of such things, the old times, their holocaust. How is it that one can turn to God and believe and be changed, but not changed enough to accept the consequences? She knew it was dealing with the consequences that would make her strong, bring her closer to her children and to God; it was perhaps what makes people good, if becoming good is ever really possible.

And maybe, just maybe, it wasn't too late for Jessie. She and Buck felt Jessie was lost to them. But starting now, she would not accept that. Starting now, she would do everything in her power to keep from losing Jessie again. She would talk to her tonight, after they got home, and this time she would enter fully into the consequences of Jessie's rage and contempt.

She found Pooh on the back porch, tossing pebbles toward the woodshed and waiting to walk her to the barn where Buck was helping Willie.

'I'm so sorry.' The breath was raked out of her.

'What for, Mama?'

'For everything.'

She went to him and put her arms around him. Her seventeen-year-old son, her dear Pooh—the one she had 'kept,' if it could be called keeping.

He looked into her eyes, unafraid, and listened.

'For all the times I neglected you and left you and didn't look after you and love you enough.' She tried to hold it back, but she could not, she could not.

'That's okay, Mama.' He patted her shoulder. 'You can stop crying if you want to. It's okay.'

Lace prayed on her walk to the barn with Dooley and Jack Tyler. Maybe Sammy and Kenny and Pauline would just avoid one another or maybe there would be some kind, any kind, of healing. Just a start would be a relief.

She had never had a problem with drinking, but she knew how it worked, she had lived with it. It was demons unloosed, it was total craziness and consuming bondage and she understood the pain of that bondage. But she was weary of Pauline clinging to the role of victim.

Pauline and Buck were standing outside the entrance to the shed. She had always embraced Pauline first; she was startled when Pauline embraced her.

'I'm so happy for you,' said Pauline, realizing suddenly that she was also happy for herself and Buck and all her children, if only for this fleeting moment. She embraced Dooley and felt his reserve and stood away and pressed his hand. 'So proud of you,' she said. She hoped to speak with him before the evening ended and was surprised to find that she looked forward to it, was eager for it. Her mission, after all, was to acknowledge and confess, she was not seeking miracles.

He saw Pauline smile as she took Jack Tyler's hands and looked into his upturned face.

'The dam has burst,' he said to Cynthia. 'It will soon

overflow the banks and water the dry land for the harvest to come.'

She assumed he was talking about the long-awaited wedding and was amused by what sounded like the proclamation of Jeremiah on a good day. It was his special white vestments, of course—after a stint in all that brocade and gold trim, he could on occasion sound positively biblical.

Dooley squatted and patted his shoulder. 'Climb up here,' he said to Jack Tyler. He liked the feel of his son's sturdy legs on his shoulders, the heft of this boy. Dooley stood then and took his wife's hand. 'Ready?'

'Here we go,' she said.

'Here we go!' said Jack Tyler, holding on.

The lanterns, so many!—even along the rafters, and the candle flames dancing against the shade of evening. The roses, the great masses of Seven Sisters everywhere, and the long table with its double rows of fancy napkins and shining plates and sparkling glasses and the miniature hand-carved replica of Choo-Choo at every place.

This is what they had worked for, prayed for, dreamed of. And here it was, with everyone happy and cheering and clapping as they entered the shed—all of it so much more than they could have imagined.

'Everything looks so beautiful, so perfect,' Lace said to Lily.

Lily was in recovery from a scene in the kitchen that involved her sisters. *No*, Violet could not sing with the band, she had not been *invited* to sing with the band, what was she *thinking?* Then Arbutus requested leftovers to take home to her brick house with a screened porch, which was the most outrageous thing she ever heard of. *Leftovers*, she said, are what this couple will be *livin'* on for days to come, give me a *break*. Then Rose's back went out because she wore the wrong shoes.

This coming Friday, thanks to a very thoughtful gift from the new Miz Kavanagh, she was drivin' to Myrtle Beach—totally alone!—where she would lie in th' sun an' ruin her skin and get her head back together.

'I recommend th' barbecue,' Lily told the bride. 'Th' coleslaw's to die for, you want th' deviled eggs on th' yellow platter not th' other platter, an' Miss Louella's biscuits are blue ribbon. As for th' chicken—so-so. But don't bother, I'll fix y'all's plates right now, before th' band rolls in.'

Lace kissed her on the cheek. 'You're the best,' she said.

Lily had been watching the busy little woman in spike heels and goofy glasses. She was a worker, all right.

'Get you a plate,' said Lily.

'Oh, I'm not a guest,' said Vanita. 'Just, you know, a professional—gettin' ready to pack up an' go home.'

Lily smiled, which she realized felt good to her face. 'We do takeout,' she said, loading barbecue and all the trimmings on a paper plate.

Mary Ellen Middleton had never met a cleric with such a lot of physical mien. Not that clerics didn't have muscle and all that—surely they did, some of them, anyway. And not that his physique was overdone, not at all. Just—robust, perhaps, though that sounded like a Cabernet. Father Brad was different. He didn't smell of church, if one could say what such a smell would be, but of something light and moving that couldn't be caught or confined.

When they met earlier today at the fence, she made conversation as best she could, based on what she'd heard. 'So I hear you have . . . lived in the wild?'

Oh, what laughter he had. He was brimming with it, absolutely running over.

'I'm no John the Baptist,' he said, 'but yes, I like the outdoors. You can ask Sammy Barlowe about that. And you?'

'I've had my nose in a book most of my life. Except during summers at the lake when we took out the canoes, and I was on a swimming team in college. And I love fishing, come to think of it.'

'Trout? Salmon? Marlin?'

'Crappie,' she had said, amused.

Just two minutes ago, she had looked for him among the chattering throng at the food tables and saw him talking with Father Tim's brother.

Yet as soon as she took her plate to the table and sat down, he popped into the chair next to her, with his own plate. How did he do that? Perhaps clergy had a knack for being everywhere at once.

'Wonderful wedding!' he said, putting the napkin in his lap. 'Memorable in every way, to say the least. Thanks in part to Beth, who is a wonder.'

'She is, I agree. Thank you.' She felt suddenly shy with him, though they had talked earlier about his deceased wife and his daughters and grandchildren and she had spoken briefly of Paul. He had brought out his cell phone and scrolled away until he was able to show pictures that she could barely see because of the glare. Everyone did that these days, she couldn't understand it.

He looked at her and smiled. He was very direct and very nice-looking. If she had to find just one word for him, it would be *vivid*. No blur. Sharp contrast. Alive. She hadn't felt really alive since Paul.

'What's your schedule?' he said, tucking into the barbecue.

'To the hotel in Wesley tonight and back to Boston in the morning.'

'May I ask who you're going back to?'

'My eighty-four-year-old mother, still living on her own. My piano; my cat, Sofia; my orchids.'

'Orchids! They never rebloom for me. I'm a nut for gardenias.'

'I love gardenias,' she said. 'But they're so finicky.'

'Completely. You never know where you stand with a gardenia. With a geranium, yes. With a pot of ivy, cool. But gardenias? It's easier to raise teenagers. Nevertheless, I'm hooked.'

'Then there's the maidenhair fern,' she said.

Clearly he enjoyed laughing.

'So, Mary Ellen, I ask you—why are we talking about houseplants? I'd rather know if you like your fries with ketchup or aioli, whether you've ever rafted the Colorado River or fried trout beside a stream in Montana. In the morning, you'll be flying to Boston and I will be . . .' He looked up to the rafters, as if seeking words.

She was smiling. 'You will be . . . ?'

'Bereft!'

She laughed.

He didn't know how he said this stuff. He never said this stuff. He was outgoing in the pulpit, outgoing on a raft with a berserk youth group or asking the parish for money if absolutely necessary. He was, however, notoriously shy around beautiful women.

Kate had been gone eight years and there had been nobody since; his Marine Corps motto had applied there, too. Kate had been the love of his life and now, out of the blue, here was somebody else he didn't want to let go.

'Okay, you were hungry, so let's eat,' she said. She held out the forkful of baked beans. He shook his head.

'A deviled egg, then. I just ate one, they're delicious.' No.

She knew about trying to get kids to eat, a bonus learning curve from the nonprofit art school. Most of them devoured their free lunch, but some were in a lot of emotional pain and ate like birds. She had been there, done that, got the T-shirt, as Lonnie would say.

'Are you worried about something?'

He was quiet for a moment. 'Am I bein' good?'

'Oh, yes!' She was startled. 'You're being very good.' Amazingly good, considering all that was going on now and all that had happened before. 'Why?'

He couldn't answer that. He just wondered if he stopped being good and started being bad, what would happen? Would it still be forever? Sometimes he was bad and couldn't help it.

'Come sit on my lap,' she said. Soon, very soon, he would think himself too big for lap-sitting. He got down from his chair and she picked him up; he was solid as anything. She held him close and swayed her body a little, like a cradle rocking, and soon he looked at her with the lovely solemnity that seemed a hallmark of their Jack Tyler, and said, 'I could prob'ly have a deviled egg now.'

And there came Dooley with Sammy and Kenny and Julie and Etta and Ethan and Pooh and Jessie, and they would all sit together as family. Happiness. So much of it, all at once. And no, she mustn't be frightened of grace. She must let God give her all this and she must receive it with a glad heart.

'Sunset, seven forty-five!' called Willie, passing among the crowd under the shed. 'Right yonder!' He pointed west.

He was the old lamplighter, going his rounds, announcing the way of things in this world in case anybody was interested. All they had to do was turn around and look. But maybe people didn't care about how the sun set behind the mountains and how the mountains turned deep blue, then black as coal after the sun was gone, which made a person think if a person cared about thinking. All that sight to see, and then the stars coming out. It was a miracle he had appreciated all the days of his life.

He was putting together a nice dinner for the barn cats and the new kittens when he noticed a little handful of guests havin' a look. Harley and his Miss Pringle, for one, and Kenny and his young family, and Father Tim, he liked a sunset and so did his wife, an' the woman from Boston, she turned around and the other preacher in a collar, he did, too, and Miss Agnes from up th' holler and her boy who did the carvings, they turned around. You could tell a lot about people who would stop what they were doin' to watch the Almighty go about his business.

Helene Pringle was looking smart, he thought. He was fortunate to have such a tenant in the rectory, which he had owned for some years.

'Helene! We're glad you could join us.' She had patiently endured Sammy Barlowe's rude behavior years ago, and Kenny's long bunk-in with Harley.

'I've missed you and Cynthia being next door,' she said. 'And Mr. Welch living downstairs. And of course, dear Barbizon, just a month ago, *il est mort*.'

'He was a very amiable cat.'

'Twenty-one years.'

'It gets better with time.' All he seemed able to summon was a platitude, albeit well-meant. 'I wish you could have seen our friend Harley being chased by the bull. He went into the field at the age of sixty-seven and came over the fence looking twenty-nine.'

She smiled. '*Adrenaline*, Father. It's cosmetic.'

Ironically, Helene Pringle had given him one of the great adrenaline rushes of his life—the day they drove down the mountain in her vintage car with next-to-zero brakes.

Twenty-one years. He gave her a hug.

'You'll be alone no more, Helene. We'll be home tonight with a car full—and there goes the neighborhood.'

'So, anybody in this group going to make a toast?' said Dooley. Bowser nosed his leg, looking for a scrap.

'Not me,' said Pooh.

'Sam?'

'Hey, I'm happy for you guys, I love you, that's m-my speech.'

'We'll take it. Ken?'

'God is good. End of discussion.'

Laughter, high fives. And there was Bonemeal giving him a look.

'How about you, Jess?'

She shrugged, looked away.

So, okay, speaking was not his primary skill, but somebody had to do it. 'I'm in.'

'Yay, Doc!' said Lace.

'Yay, Doc!' said Jack Tyler, who was digging into Honey Hershell's creamed corn.

'Game on, dude.' Sam tapped his knife against a glass.

The sun went down, the groom stood up. He didn't want to be bawling in front of people like his dad was so famous for doing. But this was a roller coaster, all this simple country wedding business and Jack Tyler coming; he was knocked out by it, crazy with feelings he was usually able to keep under control. What do you do with that kind of stuff when you stand up in front of people? What if it all came busting out in everybody's face like Choo-Choo? But come on, he was a husband now, he was a dad, he was a licensed vet—let it roll, he could do this.

'Thanks, everybody, for coming out to be happy with us!'

Cheers, applause. Cowbell.

'And thanks for all the great cooking. Lace and I couldn't have done this without you, that's for sure.

'I'd like to make a few tributes, but I'm going to let you off the hook, so no need to clap till the end unless you can't help yourself.'

Laughter. Cowbell. Scattered applause from those who couldn't help themselves.

'We thank our parents, who have done everything they could to help us get settled, who stood by us even when we were crazy, and were always there for us. Dad, Cynthia, Doc, Olivia . . . call on us anytime. We're here for you, too.

'Which reminds me, Dad—you're goin' to need a truck. When you're ready, give me a shout, I'm your man.

'Thanks to my brother Sammy, who flew in from a big competition in Minneapolis, where he hammered his three-rail bank shot in the last game and won the championship!'

Cowbell, applause. 'Way to go, Sam!' shouted Doc Owen.

'Thanks to my brother Kenny, who came from Oregon with his wife, Julie, and their two kids. Ethan and Etta have given Jack Tyler a really priceless gift—instant cousins!'

Cowbell, applause; clearly, people had no desire to help themselves.

'Thanks to my brother and sister, who came all the way from Mitford—thumbs up with th' dogs, Jess, good job bein' best man, Pooh. Y'all made a difference.'

Cowbell, applause. 'Pooh! Jess! Yo!'

'Thanks to my dad's brother, Uncle Henry, a railroad man from Mississippi who rode the Crescent up from Birmingham, and to Uncle Walter and Katherine, here from New Jersey.

'Where's Father Brad? We appreciate you being part of the

ceremony and for being such a great influence in our lives. I can hardly wait for the next snow camp mash-up in a high wind, followed by nosebleed and a great meal out of a can.'

Laughter, applause, cowbell.

'Thanks, Beth, for coming down from New York and singing for us and helping Lace, and thank you, Mary Ellen, for joining us from Boston. We appreciate it.'

Applause, cowbell.

He held up the small carving of a bull, the neck tied with raffia. 'Great job, Clarence. Thanks for the amazingly lifelike images of the big guy who made our wedding unforgettable.'

Applause. Cowbell.

'Thumbs up to the Ham Biscuits, who are really great musicians and special friends. Thanks, guys, for totaling the tenderloin before we could get to it. And special thanks for saving our gizzards.'

'Gizzards!' said Jack Tyler.

Whistles, applause. 'Go, Biscuits!' Cowbell.

'To all of you who unloaded your scraps under the table, even though their vet has all four canines strictly on kibble—thanks for ruining my game. And thanks, Danny, for giving me the opportunity to kiss the bride. Think I'll do it again.' He leaned down and did it again.

'Go, D-Do-Right!'

Applause with cowbell.

'That was a crowd-pleaser,' Doc Owen said to the table.

'Okay,' said Dooley. 'This is a big one. Somebody—we don't know who—made it possible for Kenny and Julie and

Ethan and Etta to fly from Oregon. This means a lot to our family, we truly appreciate it. So come on, people, let us know who you are. Maybe you'll stand.'

He expected Doc and Olivia to stand, even though they wouldn't especially like doing it.

But nobody stood.

'So okay, my thanking is about done.'

He stooped to Jack Tyler—'Here we go, buddy'—and picked him up and held him in the crook of his arm and felt the boy's arm slide around his neck.

Lace stood with him. Candle flames shimmered along the table.

'Lace and I thank God for giving us our son, Jack Tyler.

'It's been a long road for him and for us to get where we are tonight, and a few times we thought we wouldn't make it.

'Dad is one for the quotes; he'll throw a quote at you in a heartbeat. I don't have that talent, but when I started vet school, I did find something that worked for me. I actually wrote it on the wall of my apartment. The landlord said he'd seen worse.'

Laughter.

'I think John Lennon said it. *Everything will be okay in the end. And if it isn't okay, it isn't the end.*

'Tonight everything is better than okay. But it isn't the end. It's just the beginning.

'Here's to a new beginning, everybody. We love you.'

'Dancing on the porch!' said Lace.

Cowbell. Applause. Standing ovation. The whole nine yards.

Doc Owen gave her a kiss on the cheek. 'He could run for county supervisor and get us a two-lane bridge up the road.'

Lace laughed. 'Don't even think about it. You run for county supervisor and get us a two-lane bridge!'

She hadn't known her husband could make a talk that was so natural and fun.

'That was wonderful,' she said. 'Perfect.'

His legs were H_2O. He had blanked and couldn't remember what he said. And who did he leave out? He'd rather neuter a boar hog.

Vanita pulled the minivan onto the shoulder of the state road and foraged in the camera bag for her notebook and pen. She was almost home, which was south of Mitford and halfway to Holding, but if she didn't write this stuff down—*sayonara*.

She scribbled the headline, she could see it now.

Local Couple Says I Do,
Bull Says You Do Not!!!

She couldn't stand it another minute—the smell in here was driving her crazy. She retracted her seat belt and picked up the plate from the floor of the passenger side and peeled back the foil and so what if she didn't have a fork.

Two and a half cherry pies and two OMCs, down the hatch.

Cynthia had gone to the house; he could hear the musi‑cians tuning up on the porch. He scraped the minute remains off the two cake plates into a Ziploc.

He could not have a slice, but he could sure have crumbs. He zipped the baggie and folded it and put it in his jacket pocket.

'Rose Watson lives!' he said to Lily, though she didn't have a clue what he was talking about.

'How would you like to have some fun?'

She didn't know how to process this remark; it sounded like a pickup line that nobody used anymore.

'I know this song,' Tommy said. He was holding the sheet music Doc Harper wanted him to play tonight. 'If you'll sing it with me, we could step in the front room and do a quick run-through. Nobody's in there and we have a few minutes.'

A song she'd never heard in her life? With only a quick run-through? Just *out there*?

'I've never heard this song.'

'But would you sing it with me?'

She was going to say no, but when she opened her mouth she said, 'Yes.'

She found Dooley in the living room, waiting for Lace to come down for the first dance. Regret wasn't enough, it would never be enough.

He made eye contact with her and she was grateful.

'I'm so sorry,' she said. 'For everything.'

She tried to remember him when he was little, but she could not.

'Thanks,' he said. He waited, looking down, and then up again. 'It's okay.'

She understood that this was all he had to say. He said it was okay, not in the same way Pooh meant it, but in a good way.

He watched her turn and walk out to the porch and wanted to go after her and give her something more, but he couldn't. As a child, he had loved her desperately, no matter what, the way God loved him, no matter what. He was glad she said something from a place beneath the surface; he had felt the current of it.

It was like on TV, the way the mom looked in the shining dress and the music in the yard started playing really loud and the Tommy person was singing and people were clapping and the dad walked across the porch to the mom and then they were dancing really slow.

I set out on a narrow way many years ago
Hopin' I would find true love along the broken road . . .

The lady whose husband died and went up to heaven said that when people die everything in heaven is perfect. Everybody is happy. Maybe this was heaven, but he hoped he had not died, but if he had, he didn't know when it happened. Maybe when he ate a piece of cake tonight that made the stars go off behind his eyes and somebody said it was to die for. He felt all over himself and he was still here and not dead and his ring was here that said forever.

He wanted to be with them and not the grannies, so he ran over to where they were dancing and looked up and the dad stopped and laughed and picked him up and they all three danced together wearing rings that said something special inside and the people watching clapped again.

When they twirled around like on TV, the lights ended up being a big circle shining. And all the people watching ran together in a circle, too. He was as tall as Big Bird.

This guy in a collar, dancing with a Boston woman, was someone he didn't know. No, wait. It was someone he knew, but from a very long time ago.

Now the band was playing a number he'd heard Randy Travis sing. He liked Randy, who was somebody who had scrambled up mountains and fallen off more than a few.

They say time can play tricks on a memory

Make people forget things they knew . . .

Where to take it from here? When you're doing a big hike, you make rest stops. He had talked way too much, it was time to be quiet and listen to the words . . .

Crazy thought. That means he'd have to go home tonight and clean out his Jeep and wash it in the moonlight and remember to vacuum the seats coated with Daisy's dog hair and take the gum out of the ashtray. But tomorrow was Monday, alleluia; he could do this.

'So how about if I pick you and Beth up in the morning, we get your car back to the rental place, and I drive you to the airport?' This was going way out on a limb—a place he'd always enjoyed going, actually.

He held her closer, but only a little closer. He was clergy, after all, on view to the world twenty-four/seven.

She didn't say yes and she didn't say no. She said, 'Aioli.'

He laughed. They both laughed. He wanted to kiss this woman. Just once. Once! Surely that wasn't too much to ask—after all, she would be leaving in the morning.

When he picked her up at the hotel, he would bring her a bloom from his *Gardenia jasminoides*.

'Look,' she said to Dooley.

Hoppy and Olivia dancing. She thought they were beautiful, the way they fit together like two pieces of a jigsaw puzzle.

And there was Jack Tyler dancing with Etta and Cynthia

and Father Tim, and in the yard, Buck and Pauline dancing, and Katherine in her super-great jeans and really expensive pearls dancing with her husband of forty-nine years, and Henry smiling his lovely smile at Rebecca Jane, who had caught the bouquet even though she was joining a nunnery if she didn't get accepted at UNC.

And there was Harley sitting with Miss Pringle on a bench beneath maples lit by fireflies.

'I don't understand it,' said Dooley.

'Maybe we don't need to understand it,' she said.

Sammy and Kenny and Pooh and a few others were shooting pool, so she and Dooley danced with Julie and Jessie, and then Henry danced with Cynthia, very stately and sweet, and Rebecca Jane hauled Danny off the porch and made him dance with her.

'I don't want t' dance!' said Danny.

'Dance!' said Rebecca Jane. 'It's what you do at weddings! Show some manners, for gosh sake!'

Rebecca Jane Owen had tormented him all his life. One time when he was seven and she was twelve, he took the rungs off the ladder to her tree house and hid them in the woods. She was totally overdue . . .

'Look,' said Dooley.

Tommy had stepped away from the band and was dancing with Beth.

'Why can't life always be lived under the stars,' she said, 'with great music and family and friends?' A purely rhetorical question, but she had to wonder.

Cynthia sat with Etta on the glider while Julie went up to Heaven to put Ethan to bed. Given the innumerable books she had written and illustrated for children, she should have discovered a better opening line, but so far she had not.

'How old are you, Etta?'

'Foah.'

'You're the same age as Jack Tyler!'

'I know thith.'

'Did you see the cows?'

'Yeth.' Etta stretched her arms wide. 'Thith big.'

'And the chickens?'

'I could take one home in my duffel. I could take out my thingths and put in a chicken. He could thleep with me in my bed.'

'Do you have a dog?'

'Woolly. He thleeps in my bed.'

'Do you think Woolly and your chicken would get along?'

'If they do not get along, I would thend the chicken back.'

'I love your curly hair.'

Etta nodded. She had heard this before.

'And your dress is a dream. Very sweet with the polka dots.'

'My dreth is new.'

'Mine is old.'

'I have two old drethes.'

'Just two? I have a closetful. Well, Etta, you certainly know how to dance.'

'I wiggle mythelf all ovah.'
Cynthia laughed. 'That works!'

Nine o'clock and Tommy and the Biscuits had never sounded better; everybody was having a blast.

They had bedded their exhausted pup in a crate in Jack Tyler's room, taken off the boy's boots and helped him change into pajamas, no bath tonight. They were all wired from the dancing and the laughter and the OMC and the cherry pie. Now to wind down a four-year-old with the full moon as a major night-light.

'Did you brush your teeth?' she said. 'Over and over?'

'Not over an' over.'

'You need to do it over and over, there are germs in there.' How could she say these things that she had never been told as a child? She just opened her mouth and out came information that she supposed mothers were born to say. She would have to get more books—a lot of books.

'Does germs have teeth?'

'They do. I think they do. They can eat up your gums.' Really—how could she ever . . . ?

'Does cows have teeth?'

'They do,' said Dooley.

'Does they bite?'

'Not often. But they can. You'll get to know the heifers,

and before long, we'll be feeding them grain together. Right out of our hands.'

'Can cows git in th' house?'

'Probably not. They sleep in the pasture inside a fence. They wouldn't like being in the house.'

'Can they climb up stairs?'

'Definitely not. If they could, our pup would bark and scare 'em right out the window. But they're not going to get in the house. Unless you let them in.'

Jack Tyler laughed his quick, squealing laugh and squeezed Roo to his chest. 'I'm not lettin' no cows in th' house.'

'Good,' said Dooley. 'Glad that's settled.'

'I don't want to sleep by myself.'

'Aunt Julie will come and check on you,' said Lace. 'Cousin Etta and Cousin Ethan are right up the stairs from you. Your dad and I will check on you, and our puppy is here with you and Roo is with you and we won't go downstairs till you fall asleep.'

'Doesn't get any better than that,' said Dooley. 'How did you like being in the wedding? You did a great job. Was it fun?'

'Yeah. I like my pants.'

'We like your pants, too. How about that ring, dude? What does yours say inside? Remember?'

'Forever!'

'Don't take it off, leave it on when you wash your hands,' she said. 'As you get bigger, we'll have it expanded so it grows with you.'

'Did you like dancing with Etta?'

'She talks funny.'

'We all talk funny,' said Dooley.

Jack Tyler flopped back on the pillow and closed his eyes. They thought he might be settling down. But no. He sat up. 'I have a great idea!'

'Shoot,' said Dooley.

'We could make another wedding tomorrow!'

She loved seeing her husband laugh till his face turned red.

The laughter gave them all a second wind. Jack Tyler held up his unstuffed toy and jiggled it. 'Roo, Roo, Roo! You carried Roo!'

'I liked carrying Roo,' she said.

'Why?'

'Because you love him, I love him, too.'

'You can carry him again.'

'Thanks. Now lie down. And tomorrow we'll talk about giving our puppy a name,'

'She's already got a name,' said Jack Tyler. 'Her name is Charley.'

'Remember the puppy's a female,' said Dooley. 'How about if we give her a girl's name?'

Jack Tyler examined the buttons on his pajama top.

'Molly, Maggie, Chloe . . . ?' said Dooley.

'Just Charley. That's her name.'

'Is that what you named her?'

Jack Tyler sighed. 'Her name has always been Charley.'

Dooley looked at Lace, who was looking at the child come into their lives. 'What do you think?'

'I think her name is Charley,' she said.

She combed Jack Tyler's tousled hair with her fingers. After the dance with her dad, she had danced with her son, who had held her hands and jumped up and down to the music and wiggled his hips and everybody applauded, in love with the little guy who had appeared to them out of the blue.

'Down you go,' she said. 'No more excuses.'

'Why?'

'It's time to sleep.'

'Why?'

'Because nighttime is when people sleep and get strong for the next day.'

'And because it's time for us to tell your story,' said Dooley.

'About th' aunts an' uncles an' cousins?'

'But only if you lie down.'

Jack Tyler squirmed under the cover and put his head on the pillow.

Her husband. Barefoot, sitting on the bed and leaning against the wall, as if he'd always done this . . .

'Uncle Sammy, Uncle Pooh, Uncle Kenny, Uncle Doc, Uncle Henry, Uncle Harley . . .'

Dooley recited the names slowly, like small waves lapping the shore.

'Which is Uncle Doc?'

'The big man with the big voice wearing the big tennis shoes.'

'Which is Uncle Henry?'

'The tall man in a dark suit with a red tie and a soft voice.'

'Now you,' said Jack Tyler.

'Aunt Jessie,' said Lace. She would draw out the syllables, lull him to sleep. 'Aunt Julie, Aunt Marge, Granny O, Granny C, Granny Pauline . . .'

'That is so many grannies for one person.' His eyelids were heavy.

'Tomorrow,' Lace said to Dooley. 'We'll start tomorrow . . .' Teaching Jack Tyler not to say *ain't*, which was a big no-no with Dooley, teaching him to say *please* and *thank you* and all the things that . . .

Jack Tyler yawned. 'Now you,' he said to the dad.

'Granpa Tim, Granpa Hoppy . . .'

'Hoppy is a bunny rabbit.'

'Granpa Buck.'

'Plus Cousin Etta,' she said. 'And Cousin Ethan, Cousin Rebecca Jane . . .'

'She's not a real cousin,' said Jack Tyler. 'She's a fake cousin.'

'So, okay,' said Dooley. 'There are a couple of other people in your story. Who am I?'

He really, really wanted to say it but he was scared to

say it but the ring said forever. So he opened his eyes. 'You're my dad.'

'And who am I?' said Lace.

He felt the laugh bubbling up inside. 'You're my mom.'

His mom and dad looked at each other and then at him and his dad kissed one side of his face and his mom kissed one side of his face and he laughed and laughed because it tickled.

'Let's pray now,' said his mom. 'Hold hands.' Jack Tyler held out his hands. He had learned this in church those times he went with the lady whose husband died and went up to heaven with the organ music.

'Dear God, we thank you for Jack Tyler and for making us a family forever. Lead, guide, and instruct us and thank you for everything about this amazing day and all the days to come . . .'

The sleeping pup rolled over in her crate at the foot of the bed.

Jack Tyler snored the nearly silent snore of childhood. Lace leaned down and kissed his forehead. She liked his sweaty, sleeping, hopeful smell of a boy come home.

The music started again; two people singing. It sounded like a CD instead of live. But it was Beth and Tommy, singing a song that she and Dooley didn't know.

I'm gonna love you like nobody's loved you
Come rain or come shine . . .

They got up from the bed and drew each other close, and in the wash of moonlight, they danced.

Honey Hershell had not danced with her husband since their own wedding, shame on them. This was heaven right here in the piney woods, and right next door to their farm. She would like to dance to this incredible band every week, but without cuttin' all that corn off the cob.

After twenty years—or was it nineteen?—she still loved her big guy. He knew how to get away with stuff nobody else could, like the Lincoln beard he was tryin' to grow and that little gold stud in his right ear and him a *cattleman*! Oh, yes, she knew exactly where Mr. Danny Do-Right got his mischief, it was from th' Hershell side.

He adjusted his collar, squinted into the mirror of the hall room, and took out his pocket comb. If nothing else, he had hair.

The band was taking a break and Mary Ellen was sitting on the porch with Agnes and Clarence and Henry and Tim and Cynthia and the New Jersey Kavanaghs.

He was probably being too forward. Then again, he didn't have forever; nobody had forever. He sat beside her and everyone was talking and he said, very discreetly, he thought, 'May I ask how long it's been since you took a stroll in the moonlight?'

'Forever and a day,' she whispered.

'How are your shoes?'

She looked at him and smiled. 'Made for strolling.'

Was she being too eager, too open? She was a little scared, her heart was racing. But he was special and she was leaving in the morning and it was only a walk . . .

He offered his arm. She took it.

'Excuse us,' he said, nodding to all, including the dogs.

They walked across the front yard and across the driveway and turned into the moonlit ribbon of the hay road, and there was the music of crickets in the grass and the singing of stars overhead.

'The light is terrible,' said Doc Harper, 'but I never got a shot of you two with Dooley's parents, so let's do it.'

She was going to remind her dad about the awkwardness of Dooley having two sets of parents, but it all happened so fast. A lot of people were in the living room during the band break, some getting ready to leave. It was a scramble. Her dad collected Father Tim and Cynthia and had backed them up to the fireplace and was fiddling with his camera. Pauline and Buck were standing only a few feet away. Why hadn't her dad thought this through?

'Mama, Buck,' said Dooley. 'Get in here.'

'Bride and groom in the middle, terrific. A set of parents either side, good, great smiles, here we go.' Flash, flash. 'Let's do it again, stand a little closer, wonderful, terrific, okay, back up another inch or two, I've got a shadow here, that's it! Lookin' good!' Flash, flash, flash . . .

'You're okay drivin' around these mountains at night? I can follow you and your mom to Wesley, make sure you're all right.'

'Really, we'll be fine,' said Beth. 'Thanks. Everything was lovely. I loved your great music. I'll love having your CDs.' She wish she hadn't said *love* so many times. She almost said she loved his voice, too; she was a wreck.

'There's something about weddings,' he said. 'They kind of shake me up. All that long road ahead—how do two people do that? Maybe it's what Bono said—marriage is like jumpin' off a tall building and discovering you can fly.'

She was flying now—looking into his kind, honest, soulful eyes, and flying.

'You comin' back anytime soon?'

'I don't know,' she said. 'I hope so. I mean, yes.' He was tall like Dooley.

'You're amazing. I like the way you sing. No tricks.'

'You don't learn many tricks singing with a choir. You have to do it without tricks. I like the way you sing, too. Really great.' Saying *really great* was insipid. You have a unique style, she might have said, or I like the way you mash the high notes . . .

She had to go, she had to finish packing, she could hardly breathe.

'I want to start playing my own stuff,' he said.

'You write, too?'

'For years. Just haven't been brave enough to put it out there.'

'You are very brave,' she said. 'It could have been Pamplona.'

He laughed. 'Thanks.' He leaned to her and kissed her cheek, and there he went, walking away like a cowboy.

She stood at the door in a kind of daze. She had never sung like that before. She had followed his lead and something happened—she had used her voice in a way that was completely unfamiliar and yet as natural as breathing. It was as if she'd long withheld a secret from herself.

When she was twelve, her voice teacher had sent a note to her parents, alluding in part to 'the remarkable gift of Elizabeth's splendid classical soprano.' Her mother had framed his monogrammed note card, written in a racing and eccentric hand; it had hung in their library for years. Classical. It was official. Tonight had been like discovering a room in her apartment that she'd never seen.

She was going inside when she heard him call her name. He was standing by the porch steps with his guitar case with the decal saying, *You want mustard with that?*

'I was just thinking. I could pick you and your mom up in the morning . . .'

Bugs smacked into lanterns. Lights shimmered in trees.

'. . . and we could drop off your rental car and . . .'

He would have to send the equipment with the guys and the extra speakers could be shoved to the back of the van to make room for whatever luggage they had. He would sweep it out tonight, definitely, and a little Armor All wouldn't hurt.

He would miss seeing Harley's truck pull into the driveway next door, and taking over the occasional soup to Helene's tenant in the basement.

'I'll miss you, buddyroe.'

'Yessir, Rev'rend, it's been a good run out here. But I'll be seein' you 'uns when I come in for supplies an' all.'

'Remember to put that book in Kenny's car for me.'

'We tried to git 'em out on Tuesday mornin' instead of afternoon, but I'm glad they won't be any planes flyin' to Oregon on that schedule, this gives 'em more . . .' Harley stopped, aghast. 'Boy howdy, I've stepped in it now.'

'Harley, Harley. You sent the tickets!'

'But don't tell nobody. Nossir, that's our little secret, you hear?'

'I hear. How in the world? I mean, did you make the reservations? How did you do that?' He couldn't possibly have made plane reservations; that took a university degree.

'Well, sir, Amber, she'd done a good bit of travelin', she done th' tickets online. I give her a nice tip.'

He breathed out. 'No more plans to visit Las Vegas?'

'Plumb over that monkey business,' he said. 'Miss Pringle wants me to lay out a garden by her back steps. I can do it m' days off.'

He gave Harley a hug with a good bit of backslapping. 'You're the best.'

'I figured this would mean a lot to Lace an' Dooley, to th' whole family. I wanted to do somethin' for everybody who's done it all for me. It started with you an' Cynthia takin' me in when I was sick as a cat an' it's went on from there, everybody pitchin' in for ol' Harley.'

'I'll pitch in for ol' Harley anytime,' he said.

What a wonder. Of all things!

'Good night, beautiful. Thanks for a wonderful day.' Her dad slipped something into her hand.

A key. A car key!

'Looks and runs like brand-new,' he said.

She had hoped for something like this, but didn't know. She loved hugging her tall, funny dad. 'Thank you, thank you, thank you!'

'Leather seats,' said her mom, 'in your favorite color.'

She also loved hugging her mom, who always smelled so good.

'With plenty of room for Jack Tyler and Charley,' said her mom, 'and only five years old!'

The Harpers, herself included, were not fans of the sleek and shining. They drove vintage stuff proudly.

'How can I ever thank you for everything you've done for me, for us?'

'Here's how,' said her dad. 'Love God, be strong, be safe, be happy.' He kissed her cheek. 'It's parked behind the wood-shed. New tires, low mileage, trailer hitch. In the long run—way better than the Caymans.'

Up ahead was a ribbon of taillights, an unusual sight on their dark country road.

'Looks like when we're leavin' th' county fair,' Mink said.

Mr. Do-Right was sleeping off his behavior in the back-seat, along with Rudy, who, quiet as any mouse, was staring out the window to see what the moon was doing.

'Maybe we should have a renewal ceremony,' said Honey.

Danny popped up from his doze. 'What's a renewal cere-mony?'

'Or maybe not,' said Honey.

'You know we'll come when needed,' he told Lace and Dooley.

'And occasionally,' said Cynthia, 'when not needed!'

He would house-sit, babysit, cattle-sit, dog-sit—you name

it. Indeed he would be volunteering to sit something for the rest of his life. It was the very job he had always wanted.

One o'clock in the morning and they were headed home to Mitford, jiggety-jog—Cynthia beside him, Walter, Katherine, and Henry in back. The Big Knot had lived up to its name in every way.

'What happened to the bourbon?' said Walter.

'Ah, yes,' he said. 'The empty bottle was fetched back for recycling by two Presbyterians, three nondenominational musicians, and one Southern Baptist. Oh, and an accidental Episcopalian.'

'Who would that be?' said Henry.

'That would be Harley, who once served time for bootlegging and didn't touch a drop of the contents!'

Their laughter was quiet and good.

'While the hole was open,' he said, 'they did another burial. The cowbell.'

'Hurray!' said his wife.

He was grateful for all the days gone by at Meadowgate— all the happiness and the many surprises. And now he was looking toward the days ahead and the happiness they would bring—with, of course, the many surprises. Some would be welcome, others not. But he would try—he really wanted to try—to welcome them all.

They met a taxi on the road, driving fast. They hardly

ever saw a taxi in these parts, and certainly not at this hour. The taxi streaked by. If he had been a gambling man, he would bet good money that Walter and Katherine's luggage was en route from the airport to Meadowgate. *C'est la vie.*

Sammy would be cooking breakfast in the morning, making, or so he promised, a 'killer' omelet. He had requested two dozen eggs they just happened to have on hand—and what better filling for an omelet than leftover ham?

He would try hard not to call Dooley in the morning, just to see how things were progressing.

Dooley and Lace stood on the glider porch and watched the taillights of the Mazda vanish along the state road. His parents had been the last to leave, reluctant, in a way. And in a way he hated to see them go. Now it was all up to them. He was ready.

'Did you see it?' she said.

'Your dad took me out to see it. You'll love it. Cup holders.'

She had never had cup holders.

'Listen,' he said. The crickets.

He recognized the great mixture of excitement and relief and fatigue surging in him.

'Amanda says he's fine, but I'm goin' across to check Homer because . . .'

'Because that's what you do,' she said, and kissed him.

She ran upstairs and looked in on Jack Tyler and Charley, who had been walked an hour ago. All was well, everybody was breathing. Then she took off her shoes and carried them next door to their new bedroom and dashed off an entry in the Dooley book.

June 14~

It is 1:30 in the morning and I am Lace Kavanagh.

Thank you, God~ it was perfect.

She slipped out of her dress and hung it on the closet door and took a quick shower and brushed her teeth and let down her long hair and put on her old nightgown that she had ironed yesterday and turned down the bed with its clean, starched sheets and went barefoot to answer the small knock at the door.

Dooley was carrying the beat-up overnight bag he had carried on weekends through college and vet school, and looking vulnerable and faintly embarrassed.

'Hey,' said Dooley.

She caught her breath. 'Hey, yourself,' she said.

ACKNOWLEDGMENTS

~

Heartfelt thanks to:

Chris Pepe, my involved, discerning, and creative editor.

Dr. Tim Short, who generously provided exactly what I needed of medical wisdom and fact; Woody Baker, seasoned cattleman and cheering section; Tammy Cody, generous spirit and tireless mother of four forever children; Merry F. Thomasson, beloved wedding planner/coordinator and apostle of grace; Nancy Bass, acclaimed painter of creatures great and small in the rural Virginia landscape; and Jerry Torchia, award-winning ad man and dear friend.

Dr. Diane Snustad; Carolyn Schaefer; Amanda Smith; Lucas Shaffer; Lee French; Randy Setzer; Eleanor Birle; Brad Van Lear; Will Lankenau; Christopher Hays; Tripp Stewart, VMD; and the outstanding staffs of Greenbrier Emergency Animal Hospital, Virginia Veterinary Specialists, and Animal Hospital of Ivy Square, all of Charlottesville, Virginia.